YEARLING BOOKS/YOUNG YEARLINGS/YEARLING CLASSICS are designed especially to entertain and enlighten young people. Patricia Reilly Giff, consultant to this series, received her bachelor's degree from Marymount College and a master's degree in history from St. John's University. She holds a Professional Diploma in Reading and a Doctorate of Humane Letters from Hofstra University. She was a teacher and reading consultant for many years, and is the author of numerous books for young readers.

For a complete listing of all Yearling titles,
write to Dell Readers Service,
P.O. Box 1045, South Holland, IL 60473.

Scott O'Dell

Island
of
the
Blue
Dolphins

A YEARLING BOOK

Published by
Bantam Doubleday Dell Books for Young Readers
a division of
Bantam Doubleday Dell Publishing Group, Inc.
1540 Broadway
New York, New York 10036

ISBN: 0-440-22021-1

Reprinted by arrangement with Houghton Mifflin Company

Printed in the United States of America

One Previous Laurel-Leaf and Yearling Edition

June 1996

10 9 8 7 6 5 4 3 2 1

OPM

For
_____

The Russell Children

Isaac
Dorsa
Clare
Gillian
and
Felicity
and to
Eric
Cherie
and
Twinkle

I

I remember the day the Aleut ship came to our island. At first it seemed like a small shell afloat on the sea. Then it grew larger and was a gull with folded wings. At last in the rising sun it became what it really was — a red ship with two red sails.

My brother and I had gone to the head of a canyon that winds down to a little harbor which is called Coral Cove. We had gone to gather roots that grow there in the spring.

My brother Ramo was only a little boy half my age, which was twelve. He was small for one who had lived so many suns and moons, but quick as a cricket. Also foolish as a cricket when he was excited. For this reason and because I wanted him to help me gather roots and not go running off, I said nothing about the shell I saw or the gull with folded wings.

I went on digging in the brush with my pointed stick as though nothing at all were happening on the sea. Even when I knew for sure that the gull was a ship with two red sails.

But Ramo's eyes missed little in the world. They were black like a lizard's and very large and, like the eyes of a lizard, could sometimes look sleepy. This was the time when they saw the most. This was the way they looked now. They were half-closed, like those of a lizard lying on a rock about to flick out its tongue to catch a fly.

"The sea is smooth," Ramo said. "It is a flat stone without any scratches."

My brother liked to pretend that one thing was another.

"The sea is not a stone without scratches," I said. "It is water and no waves."

"To me it is a blue stone," he said. "And far away on the edge of it is a small cloud which sits on the stone."

"Clouds do not sit on stones. On blue ones or black ones or any kind of stones."

"This one does."

"Not on the sea," I said. "Dolphins sit there, and gulls, and cormorants, and otter, and whales too, but not clouds."

"It is a whale, maybe."

Ramo was standing on one foot and then the other, watching the ship coming, which he did not

2

know was a ship because he had never seen one. I had never seen one either, but I knew how they looked because I had been told.

"While you gaze at the sea," I said, "I dig roots. And it is I who will eat them and you who will not."

Ramo began to punch at the earth with his stick, but as the ship came closer, its sails showing red through the morning mist, he kept watching it, acting all the time as if he were not.

"Have you ever seen a red whale?" he asked.

"Yes," I said, though I never had.

"Those I have seen are gray."

"You are very young and have not seen everything that swims in the world."

Ramo picked up a root and was about to drop it into the basket. Suddenly his mouth opened wide and then closed again.

"A canoe!" he cried. "A great one, bigger than all of our canoes together. And red!"

A canoe or a ship, it did not matter to Ramo. In the very next breath he tossed the root in the air and was gone, crashing through the brush, shouting as he went.

I kept on gathering roots, but my hands trembled as I dug in the earth, for I was more excited than my brother. I knew that it was a ship there on the sea and not a big canoe, and that a ship could mean many things. I wanted to drop the stick and run too, but I went on digging roots because they were needed in the village.

By the time I filled the basket, the Aleut ship had sailed around the wide kelp bed that encloses our island and between the two rocks that guard Coral Cove. Word of its coming had already reached the village of Ghalas-at. Carrying their weapons, our men sped along the trail which winds down to the shore. Our women were gathering at the edge of the mesa.

I made my way through the heavy brush and, moving swiftly, down the ravine until I came to the sea cliffs. There I crouched on my hands and knees. Below me lay the cove. The tide was out and the sun shone on the white sand of the beach. Half the men from our village stood at the water's edge. The rest were concealed among the rocks at the foot of the trail, ready to attack the intruders should they prove unfriendly.

As I crouched there in the toyon bushes, trying not to fall over the cliff, trying to keep myself hidden and yet to see and hear what went on below me, a boat left the ship. Six men with long oars were rowing. Their faces were broad, and shining dark hair fell over their eyes. When they came closer I saw that they had bone ornaments thrust through their noses.

Behind them in the boat stood a tall man with a yellow beard. I had never seen a Russian before, but my father had told me about them, and I wondered, seeing the way he stood with his feet set apart and his fists on his hips and looked at the little harbor as though it already belonged to him, if he were one of those men from the north whom our people feared. I was certain of it when the boat slid in to the shore and he jumped out, shouting as he did so.

His voice echoed against the rock walls of the cove. The words were strange, unlike any I had ever heard. Slowly then he spoke in our tongue.

"I come in peace and wish to parley," he said to the men on the shore.

None of them answered, but my father, who was one of those hidden among the rocks, came forward down the sloping beach. He thrust his spear into the sand.

"I am the Chief of Ghalas-at," he said. "My name is Chief Chowig."

I was surprised that he gave his real name to a stranger. Everyone in our tribe had two names, the real one which was secret and was seldom used, and one which was common, for if people use your secret name it becomes worn out and loses its magic. Thus I was known as Won-a-pa-lei, which means The Girl with the Long Black Hair, though my secret name is Karana. My father's secret name was Chowig

5

Why he gave it to a stranger I do not know.

The Russian smiled and held up his hand, calling himself Captain Orlov. My father also held up his hand. I could not see his face, but I doubted that he smiled in return.

"I have come with forty of my men," said the Russian. "We come to hunt sea otter. We wish to camp on your island while we are hunting."

My father said nothing. He was a tall man, though not so tall as Captain Orlov, and he stood with his bare shoulders thrown back, thinking about what the Russian had said. He was in no hurry to reply because the Aleuts had come before to hunt otter. That was long in the past, but my father still remembered them.

"You remember another hunt," Captain Orlov said when my father was silent. "I have heard of it, too. It was led by Captain Mitriff who was a fool and is now dead. The trouble arose because you and your tribe did all of the hunting."

"We hunted," said my father, "but the one you call a fool wished us to hunt from one moon to the next, never ceasing."

"This time you will need to do nothing," Captain Orlov said. "My men will hunt and we will divide the catch. One part for you, to be paid in goods, and two parts for us."

"The parts must be equal," my father said.

6

Captain Orlov gazed off toward the sea. "We can talk of that later when my supplies are safe ashore," he replied.

The morning was fair with little wind, yet it was the season of the year when storms could be looked for, so I understood why the Russian wished to move onto our island.

"It is better to agree now," said my father.

Captain Orlov took two long steps away from my father, then turned and faced him. "One part to you is fair since the work is ours and ours the risk."

My father shook his head.

The Russian grasped his beard. "Since the sea is not yours, why do I have to give you any part?"

"The sea which surrounds the Island of the Blue Dolphins belongs to us," answered my father.

He spoke softly as he did when he was angry.

"From here to the coast of Santa Barbara — twenty leagues away?"

"No, only that which touches the island and where the otter live."

Captain Orlov made a sound in his throat. He looked at our men standing on the beach and toward those who had now come from behind the rocks. He looked at my father and shrugged his shoulders. Suddenly he smiled, showing his long teeth.

"The parts shall be equal," he said.

He said more, but I did not hear it, for at that instant in my great excitement I moved a small rock, which clattered down the cliff and fell at his feet. Everyone on the beach looked up. Silently I left the toyon bushes and ran without stopping until I reached the mesa.

2

Captain Orlov and his Aleut hunters moved to the island that morning, making many trips from their ship to the beach of Coral Cove. Since the beach was small and almost flooded when the tide was in, he asked if he could camp on higher ground. This my father agreed to.

Perhaps I should tell you about our island so you will know how it looks and where our village was and where the Aleuts camped for most of the summer.

Our island is two leagues long and one league wide, and if you were standing on one of the hills that rise in the middle of it, you would think that it looked like a fish. Like a dolphin lying on its side, with its tail pointing toward the sunrise, its nose pointing to the sunset, and its fins making reefs and the rocky ledges along the shore. Whether someone did stand there on the low hills in the days when the earth was new and, because of its shape, called it the Island of the Blue Dolphins, I do not know. Many dolphins live in our seas and it may be from them that the name came. But one way or another, this is what the island was called.

The first thing you would notice about our island, I think, is the wind. It blows almost every day, sometimes from the northwest and sometimes from the east, once in a long while out of the south. All the winds except the one from the south are strong, and because of them the hills are polished smooth and the trees are small and twisted, even in the canyon that runs down to Coral Cove.

The village of Ghalas-at lay east of the hills on a small mesa, near Coral Cove and a good spring. About a half league to the north is another spring and it was there that the Aleuts put up their tents which were made of skins and were so low to the earth that the men had to crawl into them on their stomachs. At dusk we could see the glow of their fires.

That night my father warned everyone in the village of Ghalas-at against visiting the camp.

"The Aleuts come from a country far to the north," he said. "Their ways are not ours nor is their language. They have come to take otter and to give us our share in many goods which they have and which we can use. In this way shall we profit. But we shall not profit if we try to befriend them. They are people who do not understand friendship. They are not those who were here before, but they are people of the same tribe that caused trouble many years ago."

My father's words were obeyed. We did not go to the Aleut camp and they did not come to our village. But this is not to say that we did not know what they did — what they ate and in what way they cooked it, how many otter were killed each day, and other things as well — for someone was always watching from the cliffs while they were hunting, or from the ravine when they were in camp.

Ramo, for instance, brought news about Captain Orlov.

"In the morning when he crawls out of his tent he sits on a rock and combs until the beard shines like a cormorant's wing," Ramo said.

My sister Ulape, who was two years older than I, gathered the most curious news of all. She swore that there was an Aleut girl among the hunters.

"She is dressed in skins just like the men," Ulape said. "But she wears a fur cap and under the cap she has thick hair that falls to her waist."

No one believed Ulape. Everyone laughed at the idea that hunters would bother to bring their wives with them.

The Aleuts also watched our village, otherwise

they would not have known about the good fortune which befell us soon after they came.

It happened in this way. Early spring is a poor season for fishing. The heavy seas and winds of winter drive the fish into deep water where they stay until the weather is settled and where they are hard to catch. During this time the village eats sparingly, mostly from stores of seeds harvested in autumn.

Word of our good fortune came on a stormy afternoon, brought by Ulape, who was never idle. She had gone to a ledge on the eastern part of the island hoping to gather shellfish. She was climbing a cliff on the way home when she heard a loud noise behind her.

At first she did not see what had caused the noise. She thought that it was the wind echoing through one of the caves and was about to leave when she noticed silvery shapes on the floor of the cove. The shapes moved and she saw that it was a school of large white bass, each one as big as she was. Pursued by killer whales, which prey upon them when seals are not to be found, the bass had tried to escape by swimming toward shore. But in their terror they had mistaken the depth of the water and had been tossed onto the rocky ledge.

Ulape dropped her basket of shellfish and set out for the village, arriving there so out of breath that she could only point in the direction of the shore.

The women were cooking supper but all of them stopped and gathered around her, waiting for her to speak.

"A school of white bass," she finally said.

"Where? Where?" everyone asked.

"On the rocks. A dozen of them. Perhaps more than a dozen."

Before Ulape had finished speaking, we were running toward the shore, hoping that we would get there in time, that the fish had not flopped back into the sea, or that a chance wave had not washed them away.

We came to the cliff and looked down. The school of white bass was still on the ledge, glistening in the sun. But since the tide was high and the biggest waves were already lapping at the fish, there was no time to lose. One by one we hauled them out of reach of the tide. Then, two women carrying a single fish, for they were all of about the same size and heavy, we lifted them up the cliff and brought them home.

There were enough for everyone in our tribe for supper that night and the next, but in the morning two Aleuts came to the village and asked to speak to my father.

"You have fish," one of them said.

"Enough only for my people," my father answered.

13

"You have fourteen fish," the Aleut said.

"Seven now because we ate seven."

"From seven you can spare two."

"There are forty in your camp," my father replied, "and more than that of us. Besides, you have your own fish, the dried ones that you brought."

"We tire of that kind," the Aleut said.

He was a short man who only came to my father's shoulders, and he had small eyes like black pebbles and a mouth like the edge of a stone knife. The other Aleut looked very much like him.

"You are hunters," my father said. "Go and hunt your own fish if you are tired of what you are now eating. I have my people to think of."

"Captain Orlov will hear that you refuse to share the fish."

"Yes, tell him," my father said. "But also why we refuse."

The Aleut grunted to his companion and the two of them stalked off on their short legs across the sand dunes that lay between the village and their camp.

We ate the rest of the white bass that night and there was much rejoicing. But little did we know, as we ate and sang and the older men told stories around the fire, that our good fortune would soon bring trouble to Ghalas-at.

3

THE WIDE BEDS of kelp which surround our island on three sides come close to the shore and spread out to sea for a distance of a league. In these deep beds, even on days of heavy winds, the Aleuts hunted. They left the shore at dawn in their skin canoes and did not return until night, towing after them the slain otter.

The sea otter, when it is swimming, looks like a seal, but is really very different. It has a shorter nose than a seal, small webbed feet instead of flippers, and fur that is thicker and much more beautiful. It is also different in other ways. The otter likes to lie on its back in the kelp beds, floating up and down to the motion of the waves, sunning itself or sleeping. They are the most playful animals in the sea.

It was these creatures that the Aleuts hunted for their pelts.

From the cliff I could see the skin canoes darting

here and there over the kelp beds, barely skimming the water, and the long spears flying like arrows. At dark the hunters brought their catch into Coral Cove, and there on the beach the animals were skinned and fleshed. Two men, who also sharpened the spears, did this work, laboring far into the night by the light of seaweed fires. In the morning the beach would be strewn with carcasses, and the waves red with blood.

Many of our tribe went to the cliff each night to count the number killed during the day. They counted the dead otter and thought of the beads and other things that each pelt meant. But I never went to the cove and whenever I saw the hunters with their long spears skimming over the water, I was angry, for these animals were my friends. It was fun to see them playing or sunning themselves among the kelp. It was more fun than the thought of beads to wear around my neck.

This I told my father one morning.

"There are scarcely a dozen left in the beds around Coral Cove," I said. "Before the Aleuts came there were many."

"Many still live in other places around the island," he replied, laughing at my foolishness. "When the hunters leave they will come back."

"There will be none left," I said. "The hunters

will kill them all. This morning they hunt on the south. Next week they move to another place."

"The ship is filled with pelts. In another week the Aleuts will be ready to go."

I was sure that my father thought they would leave soon, for two days before he had sent some of our young men to the beach to build a canoe from a log which had drifted in from the sea.

There are no trees on the island except the small ones stunted by the wind. When a log came ashore, as happened once in a long time, it was always carried to the village and worked on where a chance wave could not wash it away. That the men were sent to hollow out the log in the cove, and to sleep beside it during the night, meant that they were there to watch the Aleuts, to give the alarm should Captain Orlov try to sail off without paying us for the otter skins.

Everyone was afraid he might, so besides the men in the cove who watched the Aleut ship, others kept watch on the camp.

Every hour someone brought news. Ulape said that the Aleut woman spent a whole afternoon cleaning her skin aprons, which she had not done before while she had been there. Early one morning, Ramo said he had just seen Captain Orlov carefully trimming his beard so that it looked the way it did when

17

he first came. The Aleuts who sharpened the long spears stopped this work and gave all their time to skinning the otter which were brought in at dusk.

We in the village of Ghalas-at knew that Captain Orlov and his hunters were getting ready to leave the island. Would he pay us for the otter he had slain or would he try to sneak away in the night? Would our men have to fight for our rightful share?

These questions everyone asked while the Aleuts went about their preparations — everyone except my father, who said nothing, but each night worked on the new spear he was making.

4

THE ALEUTS left on a sunless day. Out of the north deep waves rolled down upon the island. They broke against the rocks and roared into the caves, sending up white sprays of water. Before night a storm would certainly strike.

Not long after dawn the Aleuts took down their skin tents and carried them to the beach.

Captain Orlov had not paid my father for the otter he had killed. So when the news came that the hunters had packed their tents, all of our tribe left the village and hurried toward Coral Cove. The men with their weapons went first and the women followed. The men took the trail that led to the beach, but the women hid themselves among the brush on the cliff.

Ulape and I went together far out on the ledge where I had hidden before when the hunters first came.

The tide was low and the rocks and the narrow beach were scattered with bundles of otter pelts. Half of the hunters were on the ship. The rest were wading into the water, tossing the pelts into a boat. The Aleuts laughed while they worked, as if they were happy to leave the island.

My father was talking to Captain Orlov. I could not hear their words because of the noise the hunters made, but from the way my father shook his head, I knew that he was not pleased.

"He is angry," Ulape whispered.

"Not yet," I said. "When he's really angry, he pulls his ear."

The men who were working on the canoe had stopped and were watching my father and Captain Orlov. The other men of our tribe stood at the foot of the trail.

The boat went off to the ship filled with otter. As it reached the ship, Captain Orlov raised his hand and gave a signal. When the boat came back it held a black chest which two of the hunters carried to the beach.

Captain Orlov raised the lid and pulled out several necklaces. There was little light in the sky, yet the beads sparkled as he turned them this way and that. Beside me, Ulape drew in her breath in excitement, and I could hear cries of delight from the women hidden in the brush.

But the cries suddenly ceased as my father shook his head and turned his back on the chest. The Aleuts stood silent. Our men left their places at the foot of the trail and moved forward a few steps and waited, watching my father.

"One string of beads for one otter pelt is not our bargain," my father said.

"One string and one iron spearhead," said Captain Orlov, lifting two fingers.

"The chest does not hold that much," my father answered.

"There are more chests on the ship," said the Russian.

"Then bring them to the shore," my father said. "You have one hundred and five bales of otter on the ship. There are fifteen here in the cove. You will need three more chests of this size."

Captain Orlov said something to his Aleuts that I could not understand, but its meaning was soon clear. There were many hunters in the cove and as soon as he spoke they began to carry the otter pelts to the boat.

Beside me Ulape was scarcely breathing. "Do you think that he will give us the other chests?" she whispered.

"I do not trust him."

"When he gets the pelts to the ship he may leave."

"It is possible."

The hunters had to pass my father to reach the boat, and when the first one approached him, he stepped in his path.

"The rest of the pelts must stay here," he said, facing Captain Orlov, "until the chests are brought."

The Russian drew himself up stiffly and pointed to the clouds that were blowing in toward the island.

"I load the ship before the storm arrives," he said.

"Give us the other chests. Then I will help you with our canoes," my father replied.

Captain Orlov was silent. His gaze moved slowly around the cove. He looked at our men standing on the ledge of rock a dozen paces away. He looked upward toward the cliff and back at my father. Then he spoke to his Aleuts.

I do not know what happened first, whether it was my father who raised his hand against the hunter whose path he barred, whether it was this man who stepped forward with a bale of pelts on his back and shoved my father aside. It all happened so quickly that I could not tell one act from the other. But as I jumped to my feet and Ulape screamed and other cries sounded along the cliff, I saw a figure lying on the rocks. It was my father and blood was on his face. Slowly he got to his feet.

With their spears raised our men rushed down across the ledge. A puff of white smoke came from the deck of the ship. A loud noise echoed against the cliff. Five of our warriors fell and lay quiet.

Ulape screamed again and flung a rock into the cove. It fell harmlessly beside Captain Orlov. Rocks showered into the cove from many places along the cliff, striking several of the hunters. Then our warriors rushed in upon them and it was hard to tell one from the other.

Ulape and I stood on the cliff, and watched helplessly, afraid to use the rocks we held lest we injure our own men.

The Aleuts had dropped the bales of otter. They drew knives from their belts and as our warriors rushed upon them the two lines surged back and forth along the beach. Men fell to the sand and rose to fight again. Others fell and did not get up. My father was one of these.

For a long time it seemed that we would win the battle. But Captain Orlov, who had rowed off to the ship when the battle started, returned with more of his Aleuts.

Our warriors were forced backward to the cliffs. There were few of them left, yet they fought at the foot of the trail and would not retreat.

The wind began to blow. Suddenly Captain Orlov and his Aleuts turned and ran to the boat. Our men did not pursue them. The hunters reached the ship, the red sails went up, and the ship moved slowly between the two rocks that guard the cove.

Once more before it disappeared a white puff of smoke rose from the deck. As Ulape and I ran along the cliff a whirring sound like a great bird in flight passed above our heads.

The storm struck us as we ran, driving rain into our faces. Then other women were running beside us and their cries were louder than the wind. At the bottom of the trail we came upon our warriors. Many had fought on the beach. Few had left it and of these all were wounded.

My father lay on the beach and the waves were already washing over him. Looking at his body I knew he should not have told Captain Orlov his secret name, and back in our village all the weeping women and the sad men agreed that this had so weakened him that he had not lived through the fight with the Aleuts and the dishonest Russian.

5

THAT NIGHT was the most terrible time in all the memory of Ghalas-at. When the fateful day had dawned the tribe numbered forty-two men, counting those who were too old to fight. When night came and the women had carried back to the village those who had died on the beach of Coral Cove, there remained only fifteen. Of these, seven were old men.

There was no woman who had not lost a father or a husband, a brother or a son.

The storm lasted two days and the third day we buried our dead on the south headland. The Aleuts who had fallen on the beach, we burned.

For many days after that the village was quiet. People went out only to gather food and came back to eat in silence. Some wished to leave and go in their canoes to the island called Santa Catalina, which lies far off to the east, but others said that there was little water on that island. In the end a council was held and it was decided to stay at Ghalas-at.

The council also chose a new chief to take my father's place. His name was Kimki. He was very old, but he had been a good man in his youth and a good hunter. The night he was chosen to be chief, he called everyone together, saying:

"Most of those who snared fowl and found fish in the deep water and built canoes are gone. The women, who were never asked to do more than stay at home, cook food, and make clothing, now must take the place of the men and face the dangers which abound beyond the village. There will be grumbling in Ghalas-at because of this. There will be shirkers. These will be punished, for without the help of all, all must perish."

Kimki portioned work for each one in the tribe, giving Ulape and me the task of gathering abalones. This shellfish grew on the rocks along the shore and was plentiful. We gathered them at low tide in baskets and carried them to the mesa where we cut the dark red flesh from the shell and placed it on flat rocks to dry in the sun.

Ramo had the task of keeping the abalones safe from the gulls and especially the wild dogs. Dozens of our animals, which had left the village when their owners had died, joined the wild pack that roamed the island. They soon grew as fierce as the wild ones and only came back to the village to steal food. Each day toward evening Ulape and I helped Ramo put the abalones in baskets and carry them to the village for safekeeping.

During this time other women were gathering the scarlet apples that grow on the cactus bushes and are called tunas. Fish were caught and many birds were netted. So hard did the women work that we really fared better than before when the hunting was done by the men.

Life in the village should have been peaceful, but it was not. The men said that the women had taken the tasks that rightfully were theirs and now that they had become hunters the men looked down upon them. There was much trouble over this until Kimki decreed that the work would again be divided — henceforth the men would hunt and the women harvest. Since there was already ample food to last through the winter, it no longer mattered who hunted.

But this was not the real reason why autumn and winter were unpeaceful in Ghalas-at. Those who had died at Coral Cove were still with us. Everywhere we went on the island or on the sea, whether we were fishing or eating or sitting by the fires at night, they were with us. We all remembered someone and I remembered my father, so tall and strong and kind. A few years ago my mother had died and since then Ulape and I had tried to do the tasks she had done, Ulape even more than I, being older. Now that my father was gone, it was not easy to look after Ramo, who was always into some mischief.

It was the same in the other houses of Ghalas-at, but more than the burdens which had fallen upon us all, it was the memory of those who had gone that burdened our hearts.

After food had been stored in autumn and the baskets were full in every house, there was more time to think about them, so that a sort of sickness came over the village and people sat and did not speak, nor ever laughed.

In the spring, Kimki called the tribe together. He had been thinking, he said, during the winter and had decided that he would take a canoe and go to the east to a country which was there and which he had once been to when he was a boy. It lay many days across the sea, but he would go there and make a place for us. He would go alone, because he could not spare more of our men for the voyage, and he would return.

The day that Kimki left was fair. We all went to the cove and watched him launch the big canoe. It held two baskets of water and enough tunas and dried abalone to last many days.

We watched while Kimki paddled through the narrow opening in the rocks. Slowly he went through the kelp beds and into the sea. There he waved to us and we waved back. The rising sun made a silver trail across the water. Along this trail he disappeared into the east.

The rest of the day we talked about the journey. Would Kimki ever reach this far country about which nothing was known? Would he come back before the winter was over? Or never?

That night we sat around the fire and talked while the wind blew and the waves crashed against the shore.

6

After Kimki had been gone one moon, we began
to watch for his return. Every day someone went to
the cliff to scan the sea. Even on stormy days we
went, and on days when fog shrouded the island.
During the day there was always a watcher on the
cliff and each night as we sat around our fires we
wondered if the next sun would bring him home.

But the spring came and left and the sea was
empty. Kimki did not return!

There were few storms that winter and rain was
light and ended early. This meant that we would
need to be careful of water. In the old days the
springs sometimes ran low and no one worried, but
now everything seemed to cause alarm. Many were
afraid that we would die of thirst.

"There are other things more important to pon-
der," said Matasaip who had taken Kimki's place.

Matasaip meant the Aleuts, for it was now the

time of year when they had come before. Watchers on the cliff began to look for the red sails and a meeting was held to plan what to do if the Aleuts came. We lacked the men to keep them from landing or to save our lives if they attacked us, which we were certain they would. Plans were therefore made to flee as soon as their ship was sighted.

Food and water were stored in canoes and these were hidden on the rocks at the south end of the island. The cliffs were steep here and very high, but we wove a stout rope of bull kelp and fastened it to rocks at the top of the cliff so that it hung to the water. As soon as the Aleut ship was sighted we would all go to the cliff and let ourselves down, one at a time. We would then leave in our canoes for the island of Santa Catalina.

Although the entrance to Coral Cove was too narrow for a ship to pass through safely at night, men were sent there to watch the cove from dusk to dawn, besides those who watched during the day.

Shortly afterwards, on a night of fine moon, one of the men came running back to the village. Everyone was asleep, but his cries quickly awakened us.

"The Aleuts!" he shouted. "The Aleuts!"

It was news we expected. We were prepared for it, yet there was much fear in the village of Ghalas-at. Matasaip strode from hut to hut telling everyone to be calm and not to lose time packing things that would not be needed. I took my skirt of yucca fiber, however, for I had spent many days making it and it was very pretty, and also my otter cape.

Quietly we filed out of the village along the trail that led toward the place where our canoes were hidden. The moon was growing pale and there was a faint light in the east, but a strong wind began to blow.

We had gone no farther than half a league when we were overtaken by the man who had given the warning. He spoke to Matasaip, but we all gathered around to listen to him.

"I went back to the cove after I gave the alarm," he said. "When I got there I could see the ship clearly. It is beyond the rocks that guard the harbor. It is a smaller ship than the one which belonged to the Aleuts. The sails are white instead of red."

"Could you see anyone?" Matasaip asked.

"No."

"It is not the same ship which was here last spring?"

"No."

Matasaip was silent, pondering the news. Then he told us to go on to where the canoes were and wait for him, for he was going back. It was light now and we went quickly over the dunes to the edge of the cliff and stood there while the sun rose.

The wind grew cold, but fearing that those on the ship would see the smoke we did not start a fire, though we had meal to cook for breakfast. Instead we ate a small quantity of dried abalone, and afterwards my brother Ramo climbed over the cliff. No one had been down to the rocks since the canoes were hidden so we did not know whether they were still safe or not.

While he was gone we saw a man running across the dunes. It was Nanko, carrying a message from Matasaip. He was sweating in spite of the cold and he stood trying to catch his breath. We all waited, urging him to talk, but his face was happy and we knew that he brought good news.

"Speak!" everyone said in a chorus.

"I have been running for more than a league," he said. "I cannot talk."

"You are talking," someone said.

"Speak, Nanko, speak," cried many voices.

Nanko was having fun with us. He threw out his chest and took a deep breath. He looked around at the circle of faces as if he did not understand why everyone was staring at him.

"The ship," he said at last, saying the words slowly, "does not belong to our enemies, the Aleuts.

There are white men on this ship and they have come from that place where Kimki went when he left our island."

"Has Kimki returned?" an old man broke in.

"No, but it is he who saw the white men and told them to come here."

"What do they look like?" Ulape asked.

"Are there boys on the ship?" asked Ramo, who had come back with his mouth full of something.

Everyone seemed to be talking at once.

Nanko made his face stern, which was hard for him to do because his mouth had been cut in the battle with the Aleuts and ever since it had always seemed to smile. He held up his hand for silence.

"The ship has come for one reason," he said. "To take us away from Ghalas-at."

"To what place?" I asked.

It was good news that the ship did not belong to the Aleuts. But where would the white men take us?

"I do not know to what place," he said. "Kimki knows and he has asked the white men to take us there."

Saying no more, Nanko turned back and we followed him. We were fearful of where we were going, yet we were happy, too.

7

We took nothing with us when we thought we would have to flee, so there was much excitement as we packed our baskets. Nanko strode up and down outside the houses, urging us to hurry.

"The wind grows strong," he shouted. "The ship will leave you."

I filled two baskets with the things I wished to take. Three fine needles of whalebone, an awl for making holes, a good stone knife for scraping hides, two cooking pots, and a small box made from a shell with many earrings in it.

Ulape had two boxes of earrings, for she was vainer than I, and when she put them into her baskets, she drew a thin mark with blue clay across her nose and cheekbones. The mark meant that she was unmarried.

"The ship leaves," shouted Nanko.

"If it goes," Ulape shouted back, "it will come again after the storm."

My sister was in love with Nanko, but she laughed at him.

"Other men will come to the island," she said. "They will be far more handsome and brave than those who leave."

"You are all women of such ugliness that they will be afraid and soon go away."

The wind blew in fierce gusts as we left the village, stinging our faces with sand. Ramo hopped along far in front with one of our baskets, but before long he ran back to say that he had forgotten his fishing spear. Nanko was standing on the cliff motioning us to hurry, so I refused to let him go back for it.

The ship was anchored outside the cove and Nanko said that it could not come closer to the shore because of the high waves. They were beating against the rocks with the sound of thunder. The shore as far as I could see was rimmed with foam.

Two boats were pulled up on the beach. Beside them stood four white men and as we came down the trail, one of the men beckoned us to walk faster. He spoke to us in a language which we could not understand.

The men of our tribe, except Nanko and Chief

Matasaip, were already on the ship. My brother Ramo was there too, Nanko said. He had run on ahead after I had told him that he could not go back to the village for his spear. Nanko said that he had jumped into the first boat that left the cove.

Matasaip divided the women into two groups. Then the boats were pushed into the water, and while they bobbed about we scrambled into them as best we could.

The cove was partly sheltered from the wind, but as soon as we went through the passage between the rocks and into the sea, great waves struck us. There was much confusion. Spray flew, the white men shouted at each other. The boat pitched so wildly that in one breath you could see the ship and in the next breath it had gone. Yet we came to it at last and somehow were able to climb onto the deck.

The ship was large, many times the size of our biggest canoes. It had two tall masts and between them stood a young man with blue eyes and a black beard. He was the chieftain of the white men, for he began to shout orders which they quickly obeyed. Sails rose on the tall masts and two of the men began to pull on the rope that held the anchor.

I called to my brother, knowing that he was very curious and therefore would be in the way of the men who were working. The wind drowned my voice and he did not answer. The deck was so crowded that it was hard to move, but I went from one end of it to the other, calling his name. Still there was no answer. No one had seen him.

At last I found Nanko.

I was overcome with fear. "Where is my brother?" I cried.

He repeated what he had told me on the beach, but as he spoke Ulape who stood beside him pointed toward the island. I looked out across the deck and the sea. There, running along the cliff, the fishing spear held over his head, was Ramo.

The sails had filled and the ship was now moving slowly away. Everyone was looking toward the cliff, even the white men. I ran to one of them and pointed, but he shook his head and turned from me. The ship began to move faster. Against my will, I screamed.

Chief Matasaip grasped my arm.

"We cannot wait for Ramo," he said. "If we do, the ship will be driven on the rocks."

"We must!" I shouted. "We must!"

"The ship will come back for him on another day," Matasaip said. "He will be safe. There is food for him to eat and water to drink and places to sleep."

"No," I cried.

Matasaip's face was like stone. He was not listening. I cried out once more, but my voice was lost in the howling wind. People gathered around me, saying again what Matasaip had said, yet I was not comforted by their words.

Ramo had disappeared from the cliff and I knew that he was now running along the trail that led to the beach.

The ship began to circle the kelp bed and I thought surely that it was going to return to the shore. I held my breath, waiting. Then slowly its direction changed. It pointed toward the east. At that moment I walked across the deck and, though many hands tried to hold me back, flung myself into the sea.

A wave passed over my head and I went down and down until I thought I would never behold the day again. The ship was far away when I rose. Only the sails showed through the spray. I was still clutching the basket that held all of my things, but it was very heavy and I realized that I could not swim with it in my arms. Letting it sink, I started off toward the shore.

I could barely see the two rocks that guarded the entrance to Coral Cove, but I was not fearful. Many times I had swum farther than this, although not in a storm.

I kept thinking over and over as I swam how I would punish Ramo when I reached the shore, yet when I felt the sand under my feet and saw him standing at the edge of the waves, holding his fishing spear and looking so forlorn, I forgot all those things I planned to do. Instead I fell to my knees and put my arms around him.

The ship had disappeared.

"When will it come back?" Ramo asked. There were tears in his eyes.

"Soon," I said.

The only thing that made me angry was that my beautiful skirt of yucca fibers, which I had worked on so long and carefully, was ruined.

8

THE WIND BLEW strong as we climbed the trail, covering the mesa with sand that sifted around our legs and shut out the sky. Since it was not possible to find our way back, we took shelter among some rocks. We stayed there until night fell. Then the wind lessened and the moon came out and by its light we reached the village.

The huts looked like ghosts in the cold light. As we neared them I heard a strange sound like that of running feet. I thought that it was a sound made by the wind, but when we came closer I saw dozens of wild dogs scurrying around through the huts. They ran from us, snarling as they went.

The pack must have slunk into the village soon after we left, for it had gorged itself upon the abalone we had not taken. It had gone everywhere searching out food, and Ramo and I had to look hard to find enough for our supper. While we ate beside a small fire I could hear the dogs on the hill not far away, and through the night their howls came to me on the wind. But when the sun rose and I went out of the hut, the pack trotted off toward its lair which was at the north side of the island, in a large cave.

That day we spent gathering food. The wind blew and the waves crashed against the shore so that we could not go out on the rocks. I gathered gull eggs on the cliff and Ramo speared a string of small fish in one of the tide pools. He brought them home, walking proudly with the string over his back. He felt that in this way he had made up for the trouble he had caused.

With the seeds I had gathered in a ravine, we had a plentiful meal, although I had to cook it on a flat rock. My bowls were at the bottom of the sea.

The wild dogs came again that night. Drawn by the scent of fish, they sat on the hill, barking and growling at each other. I could see the light from the fire shining in their eyes. At dawn they left.

The ocean was calm on this day and we were able to hunt abalone among the rocks. From seaweed we wove a rough basket which we filled before the sun was overhead. On the way home, carrying the abalone between us, Ramo and I stopped on the cliff. The air was clear and we could look far out to sea in the direction the ship had gone.

"Will it come back today?" Ramo asked.

It may," I answered him, though I did not think so "More likely it will come after many suns, for the country where it has gone is far off."

Ramo looked up at me. His black eyes shone.

"I do not care if the ship never comes," he said.

"Why do you say this?" I asked him.

Ramo thought, making a hole in the earth with the point of his spear.

"Why?" I asked again.

"Because I like it here with you," he said. "It is more fun than when the others were here. Tomorrow I am going to where the canoes are hidden and bring one back to Coral Cove. We will use it to fish in and to go looking around the island."

"They are too heavy for you to put into the water."

"You will see."

Ramo threw out his chest. Around his neck was a string of sea-elephant teeth which someone had left behind. It was much too large for him and the teeth were broken, but they rattled as he thrust the spear down between us.

"You forget that I am the son of Chowig," he said.

"I do not forget," I answered. "But you are a small son. Someday you will be tall and strong and then you will be able to handle a big canoe."

"I am the son of Chowig," he said again, and as he

spoke his eyes suddenly grew large. "I am his son and since he is dead I have taken his place. I am now Chief of Ghalas-at. All my wishes must be obeyed."

"But first you must become a man. As is the custom, therefore, I will have to whip you with a switch of nettles and then tie you to a red-ant hill."

Ramo grew pale. He had seen the rites of manhood given in our tribe and remembered them. Quickly I said, "Since there are no men to give the rites, perhaps you will not have to undergo the nettles and the ants, Chief Ramo."

"I do not know if this name suits me," he said, smiling. He tossed his spear at a passing gull. "I will think of something better."

I watched him stride off to get the spear, a little boy with thin arms and legs like sticks, wearing a big string of sea-elephant teeth. Now that he had become Chief of Ghalas-at, I would have even more trouble with him, but I wanted to run after him and take him in my arms.

"I have thought of a name," he said when he came back.

"What is it?" I asked solemnly.

"I am Chief Tanyositlopai."

"That is a very long name and hard to say."

"You will soon learn," Chief Tanyositlopai said.
I had no thought of letting Chief Tanyositlopai

go alone to the place where the canoes were hidden, but the next morning when I awoke I found that Ramo was not in the hut. He was not outside either, and I knew then that he had gotten up in the dark and left by himself.

I was frightened. I thought of all that might befall him. He had climbed down the kelp rope once before, but he would have trouble pushing even the smallest of the canoes off the rocks. And if he did get one afloat without hurting himself, would he be able to paddle around the sandspit where the tides ran fast?

Thinking of these dangers, I started off to overtake him.

I had not gone far along the trail before I began to wonder if I should not let him go to the cliff by himself. There was no way of telling when the ship would come back for us. Until it did, we were alone upon the island. Ramo therefore would have to become a man sooner than if we were not alone, since I would need his help in many ways.

Suddenly I turned around and took the trail toward Coral Cove. If Ramo could put the canoe in the water and get through the tides that raced around the sandspit, he would reach the harbor when the sun was tall in the sky. I would be waiting on the beach, for what was the fun of a voyage if no one were there to greet him?

i put Ramo out of my mind as I searched the rocks for mussels. I thought of the food we would need to gather and how best to protect it from the wild dogs when we were not in the village. I thought also of the ship. I tried to remember what Matasaip had said to me. For the first time I began to wonder if the ship would ever return. I wondered about this as I pried the shells off the rocks, and I would stop and look fearfully at the empty sea that stretched away farther than my eyes could reach.

The sun moved higher. There was no sign of Ramo. I began to feel uneasy. The basket was filled and I carried it up to the mesa.

From here I looked down on the harbor and farther on along the coast to the spit that thrust out like a fishhook into the ocean. I could see the small waves sliding up the sand and beyond them a curving line of foam where the currents raced.

I waited on the mesa until the sun was overhead. Then I hurried back to the village, hoping that Ramo might have come back while I was gone. The hut was empty.

Quickly I dug a hole for the shellfish, rolled a heavy stone over the opening to protect them from the wild dogs, and started off toward the south part of the island.

Two trails led there, one on each side of a long

sand dune. Ramo was not on the trail I was traveling and, thinking that he might be coming back out of sight along the other one, I called to him as I ran. I heard no answer. But I did hear, far off, the barking of dogs.

The barking grew louder as I came closer to the cliff. It would die away and after a short silence start up again. The sound came from the opposite side of the dunes, and leaving the trail I climbed upward through the sand to its top.

A short distance beyond the dune, near the cliff, I saw the pack of wild dogs. There were many of them and they were moving around in a circle.

In the middle of the circle was Ramo. He was lying on his back, and had a deep wound in his throat. He lay very still.

When I picked him up I knew that he was dead. There were other wounds on his body from the teeth of the wild dogs. He had been dead a long time and from his footsteps on the earth I could see that he had never reached the cliff.

Two dogs lay on the ground not far from him, and in the side of one of them was his broken spear.

I carried Ramo back to the village, reaching it when the sun was far down. The dogs followed me all the way, but when I had laid him down in the hut, and came out with a club in my hand, they trotted off to a low hill. A big gray dog with long curling hair and yellow eyes was their leader and he went last.

It was growing dark, but I followed them up the hill. Slowly they retreated in front of me, not making a sound. I followed them across two hills and a small valley to a third hill whose face was a ledge of rock. At one end of the ledge was a cave. One by one the dogs went into it.

The mouth of the cave was too wide and high to fill with rocks. I gathered brush and made a fire, thinking that I would push it back into the cave. Through the night I would feed it and push it farther and farther back. But there was not enough brush for this.

When the moon rose I left the cave and went off through the valley and over the three hills to my home.

All night I sat there with the body of my brother and did not sleep. I vowed that someday I would go back and kill the wild dogs in the cave. I would kill all of them. I thought of how I would do it, but mostly thought of Ramo, my brother.

9

I DO NOT remember much of this time, except that many suns rose and set. I thought about what I was going to do now that I was alone. I did not leave the village. Not until I had eaten all of the abalones did I leave and then only to gather more.

Yet I do remember the day that I decided I would never live in the village again.

It was a morning of thick fog and the sound of far-off waves breaking on the shore. I had never noticed before how silent the village was. Fog crept in and out of the empty huts. It made shapes as it drifted and they reminded me of all the people who were dead and those who were gone. The noise of the surf seemed to be their voices speaking.

I sat for a long time, seeing these shapes and hearing the voices, until the sun came out and the fog vanished. Then I made a fire against the wall of the house. When it was burned to the earth I started a fire in another house. Thus, one by one, I destroyed them all so that there were only ashes left to mark the village of Ghalas-at.

There was nothing to take away with me except a basket of food. I therefore traveled fast and before night fell I reached the place where I had decided to live until the ship returned.

This place lay on a headland a half league to the west of Coral Cove. There was a large rock on that headland and two stunted trees. Behind the rock was a clear place about ten steps across, which was sheltered from the wind, from which I could see the harbor and the ocean. A spring of water flowed from a ravine nearby.

That night I climbed onto the rock to sleep. It was flat on top and wide enough for me to stretch out. Also it was so high from the ground that I did not need to fear the wild dogs while I was sleeping. I had not seen them again since the day they had killed Ramo, but I was sure they would soon come to my new camp.

The rock was also a safe place to store the food I had brought with me and everything I should gather. Since it was still winter and any day the ship might return, there was no use to store food I would not need. This gave me time to make weapons to protect myself from the dogs, which I felt would sometime attack me, to kill them all, one by one.

I had a club I found in one of the huts, but I needed a bow and arrows and a large spear. The spear which I had taken from the slain dog was too small. It was good for spearing fish and little else.

The laws of Ghalas-at forbade the making of weapons by women of the tribe, so I went out to search for any that might have been left behind. I went first to where the village had been and sifted the ashes for spearheads, and then, finding none, to the place where the canoes were hidden, believing that weapons might have been stored there with the food and water.

I found nothing in the canoes under the cliff. Then, remembering the chest the Aleuts had brought to shore, I set out for Coral Cove. I had seen that chest on the beach during the battle but did not remember that the hunters had taken it with them when they fled.

The beach was empty except for rows of seaweed washed in by the storm. The tide was out and I looked in the place where the chest had lain.

It was just below the ledge Ulape and I had stood on while we watched the battle. The sand was smooth and I dug many small holes with a stick. I dug in a wide circle, thinking that the storm might have covered it with sand.

Near the center of the circle the stick hit something hard, which I was sure was a rock, but as I dug deeper with my hands I saw it was the black lid of the chest.

All morning I worked, moving the sand away. The chest lay deep from the washing of the waves and I did not try to dig it out, but only so I could raise the lid.

As the sun rose high the tide came rushing up the beach and filled the hole with sand. Each wave covered the chest deeper until it was completely hidden. I stood on the place, bracing myself against the waves, so that I would not have to look for it again. When the tide turned I began to dig with my feet, working them down and down, and then with my hands.

The chest was filled with beads and bracelets and earrings of many colors. I forgot about the spearheads I had come for. I held each of the trinkets to the sun, turning them so that they caught the light. I put on the longest string of beads, which were blue, and a pair of blue bracelets, which exactly fitted my wrists, and walked down the shore, admiring myself.

I walked the whole length of the cove. The beads and the bracelets made tinkling sounds. I felt like the bride of a chief as I walked there by the waves.

I came to the foot of the trail where the battle had been fought. Suddenly I remembered those who had died there and the men who had brought the jewels I was wearing. I went back to the chest. For a long time I stood beside it, looking at the bracelets and the beads hanging from my neck, so beautiful and bright in the sun. "They do not belong to the Aleuts," I said, "they belong to me." But even as I said this I knew that I never could wear them.

One by one I took them off. I also took the rest of the beads from the chest. Then I walked through the waves and flung them all far away, out into the deep water.

There were no iron spearheads in the chest. I closed the lid and covered it with sand.

I looked along the bottom of the trail, but finding nothing there that I could use, gave up my search.

For many days I did not think of the weapons again, not until the wild dogs came one night and sat under the rock and howled. They were gone at daylight, but not far. During the day I could see them slinking through the brush, watching me.

That night they came back to the headland. I had buried what was left of my supper, but they dug it up, snarling and fighting among themselves over the scraps. Then they began to pace back and forth at the foot of the rock, sniffing the air, for they could smell my tracks and knew that I was somewhere near.

For a long time I lay on the rock while they trotted around below me. The rock was high and they could not climb it, but I was still fearful. As I lay there I wondered what would happen to me if I went against the law of our tribe which forbade the making of weapons by women — if I did not think of it at all and made those things which I must have to protect myself.

Would the four winds blow in from the four directions of the world and smother me as I made the weapons? Or would the earth tremble, as many said, and bury me beneath its falling rocks? Or, as others said, would the sea rise over the island in a terrible flood? Would the weapons break in my hands at the moment when my life was in danger, which is what my father had said?

I thought about these things for two days and on the third night when the wild dogs returned to the rock, I made up my mind that no matter what befell me I would make the weapons. In the morning I set about it, though I felt very fearful.

I wished to use a sea elephant's tusk for the tip of the spear because it is hard and of the right shape. There were many of these animals on the shore near my camp, but I lacked a weapon with which to kill one. Our men usually hunted them with a strong net made of bull kelp, which they threw over an animal while it slept. To do this at least three men were needed, and even then the sea elephant often dragged the net into the sea and got away.

I used instead the root of a tree which I shaped into a point and hardened in the fire. This I bound to a long shaft, with the green sinews of a seal I killed with a rock.

The bow and arrows took more time and caused me great difficulty. I had a bowstring, but wood which could be bent and yet had the proper strength was not easy to find. I searched the ravines for several days before I found it, trees being very scarce on the Island of the Blue Dolphins. Wood for the arrows was easier to find, and also the stone for the tips and the feathers for the ends of the shafts.

Gathering these things was not the most of the trouble. I had seen the weapons made, but I knew little about it. I had seen my father sitting in the hut on winter nights scraping the wood for the shafts, chipping the stones for the tips, and tying the feathers, yet I had watched him and really seen nothing. I had watched, but not with the eye of one who would ever do it.

For this reason I took many days and had many failures before I fashioned a bow and arrows that could be used.

Wherever I went now, whether to the shore when I gathered shellfish or to the ravine for water, I carried this weapon in a sling on my back. I practiced with it and also with the spear.

The dogs did not come to the camp during the time I was making the weapons, though every night I could hear them howling.

Once, after the weapons were made, I saw the leader of the pack, the one with the gray hair and the yellow eyes, watching me from the brush. I had gone to the ravine for water and he stood on the hill above the spring, looking down at me. He stood very quiet, with only his head showing over the top of a cholla bush. He was too far away for me to reach him with an arrow.

Wherever I went during the day, I felt secure with my new weapons, and I waited patiently for the time when I could use them against the wild dogs that had killed Ramo. I did not go to the cave where they had their lair since I was sure that they would soon come to the camp. Yet every night I climbed onto the rock to sleep.

After the first night I spent there, which was uncomfortable because of the uneven places in the rock, I carried dry seaweed up from the beach and made a bed for myself.

It was a pleasant place to stay, there on the headland. The stars were bright overhead and I lay and counted the ones that I knew and gave names to many that I did not know.

In the morning the gulls flew out from their nests in the crevices of the cliff. They circled down to the tide pools where they stood first on one leg and then the other, splashing water over themselves and combing their feathers with curved beaks. Then they flew off down the shore to look for food. Beyond the kelp beds pelicans were already hunting, soaring high over the clear water, diving straight down, if they sighted a fish, to strike the sea with a great splash that I could hear.

I also watched the otter hunting in the kelp. These shy little animals had come back soon after the Aleuts had left and now there seemed to be as many of them as before. The early morning sun shone like gold on their glossy pelts.

Yet as I lay there on the high rock, looking at the stars, I thought about the ship which belonged to the white men. And at dawn, as light spread across the sea, my first glance was toward the little harbor of Coral Cove. Every morning I would look for the ship there, thinking that it might have come in the night. And each morning I would see nothing except the birds flying over the sea.

When there were people in Ghalas-at I was always up before the sun and busy with many things. But now that there was little to do I did not leave the rock until the sun was high. I would eat and then go to the spring and take a bath in the warm water. Afterwards I went down to the shore where I could gather a few abalones and sometimes spear a fish for my supper. Before darkness fell I climbed onto the rock and watched the sea until it slowly disappeared in the night.

The ship did not come and thus winter passed and the spring.

10

Summer is the best time on the Island of the Blue Dolphins. The sun is warm then and the winds blow milder out of the west, sometimes out of the south.

It was during these days that the ship might return and now I spent most of my time on the rock, looking out from the high headland into the east, toward the country where my people had gone, across the sea that was never-ending.

Once while I watched I saw a small object which I took to be the ship, but a stream of water rose from it and I knew that it was a whale spouting. During those summer days I saw nothing else.

The first storm of winter ended my hopes. If the white men's ship were coming for me it would have come during the time of good weather. Now I would have to wait until winter was gone, maybe longer.

The thought of being alone on the island while so many suns rose from the sea and went slowly back into the sea filled my heart with loneliness. I had not felt so lonely before because I was sure that the ship would return as Matasaip had said it would. Now my hopes were dead. Now I was really alone. I could not eat much, nor could I sleep without dreaming terrible dreams.

The storm blew out of the north, sending big waves against the island and winds so strong that I was unable to stay on the rock. I moved my bed to the foot of the rock and for protection kept a fire going throughout the night. I slept there five times. The first night the dogs came and stood outside the ring made by the fire. I killed three of them with arrows, but not the leader, and they did not come again.

On the sixth day, when the storm had ended, I went to the place where the canoes had been hidden, and let myself down over the cliff. This part of the shore was sheltered from the wind and I found the canoes just as they had been left. The dried food was still good, but the water was stale, so I went back to the spring and filled a fresh basket.

I had decided during the days of the storm, when I had given up hope of seeing the ship, that I would take one of the canoes and go to the country that lay toward the east. I remembered how Kimki, before he had gone, had asked the advice of his ancestors who had lived many ages in the past, who had come to the island from that country, and likewise the advice of Zuma, the medicine man who held power over the wind and the seas. But these things I could not do, for Zuma had been killed by the Aleuts, and in all my life I had never been able to speak with the dead, though many times I had tried.

Yet I cannot say that I was really afraid as I stood there on the shore. I knew that my ancestors had crossed the sea in their canoes, coming from that place which lay beyond. Kimki, too had crossed the sea. I was not nearly so skilled with a canoe as these men, but I must say that whatever might befall me on the endless waters did not trouble me. It meant far less than the thought of staying on the island alone, without a home or companions, pursued by wild dogs, where everything reminded me of those who were dead and those who had gone away.

Of the four canoes stored there against the cliff, I chose the smallest, which was still very heavy because it could carry six people. The task that faced me was to push it down the rocky shore and into the water, a distance four or five times its length.

This I did by first removing all the large rocks in front of the canoe. I then filled in all these holes with pebbles and along this path laid down long strips of kelp, making a slippery bed. The shore was steep and once I got the canoe to move with its own weight, it slid down the path and into the water.

The sun was in the west when I left the shore. The sea was calm behind the high cliffs. Using the two-bladed paddle I quickly skirted the south part of the island. As I reached the sandspit the wind struck. I was paddling from the back of the canoe because you can go faster kneeling there, but I could not handle it in the wind.

Kneeling in the middle of the canoe, I paddled hard and did not pause until I had gone through the tides that run fast around the sandspit. There were many small waves and I was soon wet, but as I came out from behind the spit the spray lessened and the waves grew long and rolling. Though it would have been easier to go the way they slanted, this would have taken me in the wrong direction. I therefore kept them on my left hand, as well as the island, which grew smaller and smaller, behind me.

At dusk I looked back. The Island of the Blue Dolphins had disappeared. This was the first time that I felt afraid.

There were only hills and valleys of water around me now. When I was in a valley I could see nothing and when the canoe rose out of it, only the ocean stretching away and away.

Night fell and I drank from the basket. The water cooled my throat.

The sea was black and there was no difference between it and the sky. The waves made no sound among themselves, only faint noises as they went under the canoe or struck against it. Sometimes the noises seemed angry and at other times like people laughing. I was not hungry because of my fear.

The first star made me feel less afraid. It came out low in the sky and it was in front of me, toward the east. Other stars began to appear all around, but it was this one I kept my gaze upon. It was in the figure that we call a serpent, a star which shone green and which I knew. Now and then it was hidden by mist, yet it always came out brightly again.

Without this star I would have been lost, for the waves never changed. They came always from the same direction and in a manner that kept pushing me away from the place I wanted to reach. For this reason the canoe made a path in the black water like a snake. But somehow I kept moving toward the star which shone in the east.

This star rose high and then I kept the North Star on my left hand, the one we call "the star that does not move." The wind grew quiet. Since it always died down when the night was half over, I knew how long I had been traveling and how far away the dawn was.

About this time I found that the canoe was leaking. Before dark I had emptied one of the baskets in which food was stored and used it to dip out the water that came over the sides. The water that now moved around my knees was not from the waves.

I stopped paddling and worked with the basket until the bottom of the canoe was almost dry. Then I searched around, feeling in the dark along the smooth planks, and found the place near the bow where the water was seeping through a crack as long as my hand and the width of a finger. Most of the time it was out of the sea, but it leaked whenever the canoe dipped forward in the waves.

The places between the planks were filled with black pitch which we gather along the shore. Lacking this, I tore a piece of fiber from my skirt and pressed it into the crack, which held back the water.

Dawn broke in a clear sky and as the sun came out of the waves I saw that it was far off on my left. During the night I had drifted south of the place I wished to go, so I changed my direction and paddled along the path made by the rising sun.

There was no wind on this morning and the long waves went quietly under the canoe. I therefore moved faster than during the night.

I was very tired, but more hopeful than I had been since I left the island. If the good weather did not change I would cover many leagues before dark. Another night and another day might bring me within sight of the shore toward which I was going.

Not long after dawn, while I was thinking of this strange place and what it would look like, the canoe began to leak again. This crack was between the same planks, but was a larger one and close to where I was kneeling.

The fiber I tore from my skirt and pushed into the crack held back most of the water which seeped in whenever the canoe rose and fell with the waves. Yet I could see that the planks were weak from one end to the other, probably from the canoe being stored so long in the sun, and that they might open along their whole length if the waves grew rougher.

It was suddenly clear to me that it was dangerous to go on. The voyage would take two more days, perhaps longer. By turning back to the island I would not have nearly so far to travel.

Still I could not make up my mind to do so. The sea was calm and I had come far. The thought of turning back after all this labor was more than I could bear. Even greater was the thought of the deserted island I would return to, of living there alone and forgotten. For how many suns and how many moons?

The canoe drifted idly on the calm sea while these thoughts went over and over in my mind, but when I saw the water seeping through the crack again, I picked up the paddle. There was no choice except to turn back toward the island.

I knew that only by the best of fortune would I ever reach it.

The wind did not blow until the sun was overhead. Before that time I covered a good distance, pausing only when it was necessary to dip water from the canoe. With the wind I went more slowly and had to stop more often because of the water spilling over the sides, but the leak did not grow worse.

This was my first good fortune. The next was when a swarm of dolphins appeared. They came swimming out of the west, but as they saw the canoe they turned around in a great circle and began to follow me. They swam up slowly and so close that I could see their eyes, which are large and the color of the ocean. Then they swam on ahead of the canoe, crossing back and forth in front of it, diving in and out, as if they were weaving a piece of cloth with their broad snouts.

Dolphins are animals of good omen. It made me happy to have them swimming around the canoe, and though my hands had begun to bleed from the chafing of the paddle, just watching them made me forget the pain. I was very lonely before they appeared, but now I felt that I had friends with me and did not feel the same.

The blue dolphins left me shortly before dusk. They left as quickly as they had come, going on into the west, but for a long time I could see the last of the sun shining on them. After night fell I could still see them in my thoughts and it was because of this that I kept on paddling when I wanted to lie down and sleep.

More than anything, it was the blue dolphins that took me back home.

Fog came with the night, yet from time to time I could see the star that stands high in the west, the red star called Magat which is part of the figure that looks like a crawfish and is known by that name. The crack in the planks grew wider so I had to stop often to fill it with fiber and to dip out the water.

The night was very long, longer than the night before. Twice I dozed kneeling there in the canoe, though I was more afraid than I had ever been. But the morning broke clear and in front of me lay the dim line of the island like a great fish sunning itself on the sea.

I reached it before the sun was high, the sandspit and its tides that bore me into the shore. My legs were stiff from kneeling and as the canoe struck the sand I fell when I rose to climb out. I crawled through the shallow water and up the beach. There I lay for a long time, hugging the sand in happiness.

I was too tired to think of the wild dogs. Soon I fell asleep.

I I

I WAS AWAKENED by the waves dragging at my feet. Night had come, but being too tired to leave the sandspit, I crawled to a higher place where I would be safe from the tide, and again went to sleep.

In the morning I found the canoe a short distance away. I took the baskets, my spear, and the bow and arrows, and turned the canoe over so that the tides could not take it out to sea. I then climbed to the headland where I had lived before.

I felt as if I had been gone a long time as I stood there looking down from the high rock. I was happy to be home. Everything that I saw — the otter playing in the kelp, the rings of foam around the rocks that guarded the harbor, the gulls flying, the tides moving past the sandspit — filled me with happiness.

I was surprised that I felt this way, for it was only a short time ago that I had stood on this same rock and felt that I could not bear to live here another day.

I looked out at the blue water stretching away and all the fear I had felt during the time of the voyage came back to me. On the morning I first sighted the island and it had seemed like a great fish sunning itself, I thought that someday I would make the canoe over and go out once more to look for the country that lay beyond the ocean. Now I knew that I would never go again.

The Island of the Blue Dolphins was my home; I had no other. It would be my home until the white men returned in their ship. But even if they came soon, before next summer, I could not live without a roof or a place to store my food. I would have to build a house. But where?

That night I slept on the rock and the next day I began the search. The morning was clear, but to the north banks of clouds hung low. Before long they would move in across the island and behind them many other storms were waiting. I had no time to waste.

I needed a place that was sheltered from the wind, not too far from Coral Cove, and close to a good spring. There were two such places on the island — one on the headland and the other less than a league to the west. The headland seemed to be the more favorable of the two, but since I had not been to the other for a long time I decided to go there and make certain.

The first thing I found, which I had forgotten, was that this place was near the wild dogs' lair. As soon as I drew near to it the leader came to the opening of the cave and watched me with his yellow eyes. If I built a hut here I would first have to kill him and his pack. I planned to do this anyway, but it would take much time.

The spring was better than the one near the headland, being less brackish and having a steadier flow of water. Besides it was much easier to reach, since it came from the side of a hill and not from a ravine as the other one did. It was also close to the cliff and a ridge of rocks which would shelter my house.

The rocks were not so high as those on the headland and therefore would give me less protection from the wind, yet they were high enough, and from them I could see the north coast and Coral Cove.

The thing that made me decide on the place to build my house was the sea elephants.

The cliffs here fell away easily to a wide shelf that was partly covered when the tide came in. It was a good place for sea elephants because they could crawl halfway up the cliff if the day were stormy. On fair days they could fish among the pools or lie on the rocks.

The bull is very large and often weighs as much as thirty men. The cows are much smaller, but they make more noise than the bulls, screaming and barking through the whole day and sometimes at night. The babies are noisy, too.

On this morning the tide was low and most of the animals were far out, just hundreds of specks against the waves, yet the noise they made was deafening. I stayed there the rest of the day, looking around, and that night. At dawn when the clamor started again I left and went back to the headland.

There was another place to the south where I could have built my house, near the destroyed village of Ghalas-at, but I did not want to go there because it would remind me of the people who were gone. Also the wind blew strong in this place, blowing against the dunes which cover the middle part of the island so that most of the time sand is moving everywhere.

Rain fell that night and lasted for two days. I made a shelter of brush at the foot of the rock, which kept off some of the water, and ate the food I had stored in the basket. I could not build a fire because of the rain and I was very cold.

On the third day the rain ceased and I went out to look for things which I would need in building the house. I likewise needed poles for a fence. I would soon kill the wild dogs, but there were many small red foxes on the island. They were so numerous that I could never hope to get rid of them either by traps or with arrows. They were clever thieves and nothing I stored would be safe until I had built a fence.

The morning was fresh from the rain. The smell of the tide pools was strong. Sweet odors came from the wild grasses in the ravines and from the sand plants on the dunes. I sang as I went down the trail to the beach and along the beach to the sandspit. I felt that the day was an omen of good fortune.

It was a good day to begin my new home.

12

Many years before, two whales had washed up on the sandspit. Most of the bones had been taken away to make ornaments, but ribs were still there, half-buried in the sand.

These I used in making the fence. One by one I dug them up and carried them to the headland. They were long and curved, and when I had scooped out holes and set them in the earth they stood taller than I did.

I put the ribs together with their edges almost touching, and standing so that they curved outward, which made them impossible to climb. Between them I wove many strands of bull kelp, which shrinks as it dries and pulls very tight. I would have used seal sinew to bind the ribs together, for this is stronger than kelp, but wild animals like it and soon would have gnawed the fence down. Much time went into its building. It would have taken me longer except that the rock made one end of the fence and part of a side.

For a place to go in and out, I dug a hole under the fence just wide and deep enough to crawl through. The bottom and sides I lined with stones. On the outside I covered the hole with a mat woven of brush to shed the rain, and on the inside with a flat rock which I was strong enough to move.

I was able to take eight steps between the sides of the fence, which gave me all the room I would need to store the things I gathered and wished to protect.

I built the fence first because it was too cold to sleep on the rock and I did not like to sleep in the shelter I had made until I was safe from the wild dogs.

The house took longer to build than the fence because it rained many days and because the wood which I needed was scarce.

There was a legend among our people that the island had once been covered with tall trees. This was a long time ago, at the beginning of the world when Tumaiyowit and Mukat ruled. The two gods quarreled about many things. Tumaiyowit wished people to die. Mukat did not. Tumaiyowit angrily went down, down to another world under this world, taking his belongings with him, so people die because he did.

In that time there were tall trees, but now there were only a few in the ravines and these were small and crooked. It was very hard to find one that would make a good pole. I searched many days, going out early in the morning and coming back at night, before I found enough for the house.

I used the rock for the back of the house and the front I left open since the wind did not blow from this direction. The poles I made of equal length, using fire to cut them as well as a stone knife which caused me much difficulty because I had never made such a tool before. There were four poles on each side, set in the earth, and twice that many for the roof. These I bound together with sinew and covered with female kelp, which has broad leaves.

The winter was half over before I finished the house, but I slept there every night and felt secure because of the strong fence. The foxes came when I was cooking my food and stood outside gazing through the cracks, and the wild dogs also came, gnawing at the whale ribs, growling because they could not get in.

I shot two of them, but not the leader.

While I was building the fence and the house, I ate shellfish and perch which I cooked on a flat rock. Afterwards I made two utensils. Along the shore there were stones that the sea had worn smooth. Most of them were round, but I found two with hollow places in the center which I deepened and broadened by rubbing them with sand. Using these to cook in, I saved the juices of the fish which are good and were wasted before.

For cooking seeds and roots I wove a tight basket of fine reeds, which was easy because I had learned how to do it from my sister Ulape. After the basket had dried in the sun, I gathered lumps of pitch on the shore, softened them over the fire, and rubbed them on the inside of the basket so that it would hold water. By heating small stones and dropping them into a mixture of water and seeds in the basket I could make gruel.

I made a place for fire in the floor of my house, hollowing it out and lining it with rocks. In the village of Ghalas-at we made new fires every night, but now I made one fire which I covered with ashes when I went to bed. The next night I would remove the ashes and blow on the embers. In this way I saved myself much work.

There were many gray mice on the island and now that I had food to keep from one meal to the other, I needed a safe place to put it. On the face of the rock, which was the back wall of my house, were several cracks as high as my shoulder. These I cut out and smoothed to make shelves where I could store my food and the mice could not reach it.

By the time winter was over and grass began to

show green on the hills my house was comfortable. I was sheltered from the wind and rain and prowling animals. I could cook anything I wished to eat. Everything I wanted was there at hand.

It was now time to make plans for getting rid of the wild dogs which had killed my brother and would kill me should they ever come upon me unarmed. I needed another and heavier spear, also a larger bow and sharper arrows. To collect the material for these weapons, I searched the whole island, taking many suns to do it. This left only the nights to work on them. Since I could not see well by the dim fire I used for cooking, I made lamps of the dried bodies of little fish which we call *sai-sai*.

The *sai-sai* is the color of silver and not much bigger than a finger. On nights when the moon shines full, these little fish come swimming out of the sea in schools so thick that you can almost walk on them. They come with the waves and twist and turn on the sand as if they were dancing.

I caught many basketfuls of *sai-sai* and put them out in the sun. Hung up by their tails from the poles of the roof, they made much odor, but burned with a very clear light.

I made the bow and arrows first and was pleased when I tried them that I could shoot farther and much straighter than I had before.

The spear I left to the last. I wondered, as I

smoothed and shaped the long handle and fitted a stone collar around the end both to give the spear weight and to hold the spear point, if I could make this point the way the men of our tribe did, from the tooth of a sea elephant.

Many nights I thought about it, wondering how I could possibly kill one of these great beasts. I could not use a net of kelp, because that needed the strength of several men. Nor could I remember that a bull elephant had ever been killed with an arrow or with a spear. Only after they had been caught in a net were they killed and then with a club. We killed many cows for their oil, using spears, but the teeth were not large.

How I would do this, I did not know. Yet the more I thought about it, the greater was my determination to try, for there was nothing to be found on the island that made such good spear points as the tusklike teeth of the bull sea elephant.

13

I DID NOT sleep much the night before I went to the place of the sea elephants. I thought again about the law that forbade women to make weapons. I wondered if my arrows would go straight and, if they did, would they pierce the animal's tough hide. What if one of the bulls turned on me? What if I were injured and then had to fight the wild dogs as I dragged myself homeward?

I thought about these things most of the night, but with the sun I was up and on my way to the place where the sea elephants lived.

When I reached the cliff, the animals had left the reef and gathered along the shore. Like gray boulders the bulls sat on the pebbly slope. Below them the cows and their babies played in the waves.

Perhaps it is not right to speak of young sea elephants as babies, for they are as large as a man. But they are still babies in many ways. They follow their mothers around, waddling along on their flippers like children learning to walk, making crying sounds and sounds of pleasure that only the young make. And before they will leave the shore and learn to swim their mothers have to push them into the sea, which is often difficult to do because of their size.

Some distance separated the bulls from each other, for they are bad-tempered, very jealous by nature and quick to fight over anything that displeases them. There were six of them below me on the slope, each sitting alone like a great chief, watching his herd of cows and babies.

The cow has a smooth body and a face that looks much like that of a mouse, with a sharp-pointed nose and whiskers, but the bull is different. His nose has a large hump on it which hangs down over his mouth. His skin is rough and looks like wet earth that has dried in the sun and cracked. He is an ugly animal.

From the top of the cliff I looked down at each of the sea elephants and tried to choose the smallest of the six.

They were all the same size save one, which was the farthest from me and partly hidden by a rock. He was about half as large as the others, a young bull. Since no cows were playing among the waves in front of him, I knew that he did not have a herd of his own, and for that reason would not be so wary or quickly angered.

Quietly I let myself down over the edge of the cliff. To reach him I had to pass behind the others, being careful not to alarm them. They fear nothing and would not move if they saw me, but it was better, I thought, not to put them on their guard. I carried my new bow, which was almost as tall as I was, and five arrows.

The path was rough and covered with small stones. I took pains not to send them tumbling down the slope. I was also careful not to be seen by the cows, which get alarmed easily and would have warned the rest of the herd with their cries.

I crawled behind a big rock near the young bull. I then got to my feet and fitted an arrow to the bow although I suddenly remembered my father's warning that, because I was a woman, the bow would break.

The sun was far in the west, but luckily my shadow fell away from the young bull. The distance between us was short and his back was turned squarely toward me. Still I did not know where to place the first arrow, whether in his shoulders or in his head. The skin of the sea elephant is rough, yet very thin, but beneath it are thick layers of fat, and though his body is large, his head is small and make a poor target.

While I stood there behind the rock, not know-ing what to do, again aware of my father's warning that a bow in the hands of a woman would always break in a time of danger, the animal began to move toward the shore. At first I thought that by some chance he had heard me. I soon saw that he was on his way toward the cows that belonged to the old bull sitting nearby.

The sea elephant moves fast in spite of his size, waddling along on his great flippers which he uses like hands. The bull was nearing the water. I let the arrow go and it went straight. At the last in-stant he changed direction and, though the bow did not break, the arrow passed harmlessly to one side.

I had failed to notice that the old bull was mov-ing down the slope until I heard stones grating against each other. Quickly he overtook his rival and with a single thrust of his shoulders overturned him. The young bull stood as high as a tall man and was twice that length, yet from the force of the blow he rolled into the water and lay there stunned.

The old bull bore down upon him, swinging his head and bellowing so loud it echoed against the cliffs. The herd of cows and calves, who were lying in the waves and scratching their backs with their flippers, stopped to watch the battle.

Two of the cows were in the bull's path as he

waddled toward his rival, but he went over them as if they were small stones. Using his tusklike teeth, he ripped a long gash in the young bull's side.

The young bull raised himself and as he turned his small eyes shone fiercely red. When the old bull slashed at him again, he struck first and sunk his teeth into the other's neck. He did not let go and the two rolled over in the waves, splashing water high into the air.

The cows had scattered by now, but the other bulls still sat quietly on the slope.

The two fighters paused, getting ready for a new attack. It was a good chance to send an arrow into the young bull, who lay on his back with his teeth still grasping the other's neck. But I hoped that he would win the battle, and I stood there and did not move.

The old bull had many deep scars on his head and shoulders from battles he had fought before. Suddenly he lashed out with his tail, trying to loose the hold on his neck, and struck the side of a rock. With his tail against the rock, he flung his body out of the water and thus broke away.

He came quickly up the slope, his great mouth open, the young bull close behind him. He came toward me and, in haste to get out of his way, not knowing whether he was bent on attacking me, I stepped back. In doing so, I tripped over a stone and fell to my knees.

I felt a sharp pain in my leg, but was quickly up. By this time the old bull had whirled around and turned upon his pursuer so fast that the young bull was taken by surprise. Again the young bull's flank was ripped deep, and again the force of the blow threw him backward into the water.

The waves grew redder from his blood, but this time he rolled over and was waiting for the charge. He met the old bull with his shoulder. The sound was like rocks crashing together. Once more the young bull caught the other's throat, and together they disappeared beneath a wave. When they came up they were still locked together.

The sun had gone down and it was so dark I could no longer see clearly. My leg had now begun to hurt. Since I had a long way to go, I left them. I could hear their bellowing as I went up the cliff and for a long time afterward.

14

My leg hurt so much by the time I had reached the house that it was hard for me to crawl under the fence and move aside the heavy rock.

For five suns I could not go out because my leg had swollen so badly and I had no herbs with which to treat it. I had enough food to eat, but on the third day the water in the basket ran low. Two days later the basket was empty. It was necessary then for me to go to the spring in the ravine.

I started out when the sun rose. I took with me shellfish to eat, also my spear and my bow and arrows. I went very slowly, for I had to crawl on my hands and knees, carrying the food tied to my back, and dragging the weapons.

There was a short way to the spring, but it was over many rocks which I could not climb, so I had to take a longer way through the brush. I reached the ravine when the sun was overhead. The spring was not far off and I rested there, though I was very thirsty, cutting a lobe from a cactus bush to chew on.

While I was resting there, sucking the juice from the cactus, I saw the big gray dog, the leader of the wild pack, in the brush above me. His head was down and he was moving slowly, sniffing the tracks I had made. He saw me soon after I saw him and stopped. Behind him was the rest of the pack, trotting along one after the other. The pack stopped too.

I took up my bow and fitted an arrow, but as I did this the big dog faded away into the brush and was quickly followed by the others. In the time of one breath they were gone. There was nothing to aim my arrow at. It was as if they had not been there at all.

I listened. They were moving so silently I could not hear their steps, but I was sure that they would try to surround me. Slowly I crawled on, stopping to listen, to glance back, to measure the distance between me and the spring. My leg hurt. I left my bow and arrows behind as I went on, for the brush had grown heavy and I could not use them. In one hand I dragged my spear.

I came to the spring. It flowed out of a crack in a rock and the rock rose high on three sides of it. The wild dogs could not attack me from any of these directions, so I lay on the earth and drank, watching the ravine below me. I drank for a long time and filled my basket and then, feeling better, crawled toward the mouth of the cave.

A ledge of black rock ran out above it. Some low bushes grew there and among them, with just his head showing, stood the big gray dog. He did not move, but his yellow eyes followed me, turning slowly as I drew near the cave. Another head showed behind him and another. They were too far away for me to reach with my spear.

Suddenly I saw brush moving on the opposite bank of the ravine. The pack had split up and were waiting on both sides of the ravine for me to pass them.

The cave was now in front of me. I crawled to the mouth and into it. Above me I could hear feet running and the cracking of brush, which was followed by silence.

I was safe. I knew the wild dogs would come back and they did as night fell, stalking around in the brush until morning, but not venturing close.

Although the mouth of the cave was small, once you were inside, it spread out and you could stand up. Water dropped from the roof and the cave was cold without a fire, but here I stayed for six suns, until my leg was well, crawling out only once to fetch water from the spring.

While I was living there I decided that I would

make the cave into another house, where I could stay should I again get hurt or sick. And this I did as soon as I was strong and could walk.

The cave went far back into the hill, around many turns, but I needed only that part which lay near the opening and which the sun could reach during some of the day.

A long time before this my ancestors had used the cave, why I do not know, and along the walls on each side they had cut figures in the stone. There were figures of pelicans floating on the water and flying, of dolphins, whales, sea elephants, gulls, ravens, dogs, and foxes. Near the opening of the cave they had also cut two deep basins in the stone, which I decided to use for storing water since they held much more than the baskets.

I made shelves in the side of the rock as I had done in the other house, and gathered shellfish and seeds to store there. I also gathered herbs from the hill above the spring in case I should need them. The bow and arrows I had first made I likewise took to the cave. At the last, after I had made a good bed of seaweed and collected dry wood for my fires, I closed the opening with stones, except for a small hole at the top which I could crawl through.

All this I did, thinking of the days I had been sick and without water. It was hard work, much of it a man's work, but not until I was finished did I ge back to the place where the sea elephants lived.

The tide was low when I reached it. Far up on the slope lay the body of the old bull. Gulls had picked his bones clean, but I found what I had come for.

Some of the teeth were as long as my hand and half its width. They were curved at the tops and some were broken, but when I had ground the best of them down with sand, I had for my work four good spear points, broad at the bottom and very sharp at the ends.

I made two more spears from these points and at last was ready to go to the cave of the wild dogs.

15

There had been wild dogs on the Island of the Blue Dolphins as long as I remember, but after the Aleuts had slain most of the men of our tribe and their dogs had left to join the others, the pack became much bolder. It spent the nights running through the village and during the day was never far off. It was then that we made plans to get rid of them, but the ship came and everyone left Ghalas-at.

I am sure that the pack grew bolder because of their leader, the big one with the thick fur around his neck and the yellow eyes.

I had never seen this dog before the Aleuts came and no one else had, so he must have come with them and been left behind when they sailed away. He was a much larger dog than any of ours, which besides have short hair and brown eyes. I was sure that he was an Aleut dog.

Already I had killed four of the pack, but there were many left, more than in the beginning, for some had been born in the meantime. The young dogs were even wilder than the old ones.

I first went to the hill near the cave when the pack was away and collected armloads of brush which I placed near the mouth of their lair. Then I waited until the pack was in the cave. It went there early in the morning to sleep after it had spent the night prowling. I took with me the big bow and five arrows and two of the spears. I went quietly, circling around the mouth of the cave and came up to it from the side. There I left all of my weapons except one spear.

I set fire to the brush and pushed it into the cave. If the wild dogs heard me, there was no sound from them. Nearby was a ledge of rock which I climbed, taking my weapons with me.

The fire burned high. Some of the smoke trailed out over the hill, but much of it stayed in the cave. Soon the pack would have to leave. I did not hope to kill more than five of them because I had only that many arrows, but if the leader was one of the five I would be satisfied. It might be wiser if I waited and saved all my arrows for him, and this I decided to do.

None of the dogs appeared before the fire died. Then three ran out and away. Seven more followed and a long time afterwards a like number. There were many more still left in the cave.

The leader came next. Unlike the others, he did not run away. He jumped over the ashes and stood at the mouth of the cave, sniffing the air. I was so close to him that I could see his nose quivering, but he did not see me until I raised my bow. Fortunately I did not frighten him.

He stood facing me, his front legs spread as if he were ready to spring, his yellow eyes narrowed to slits. The arrow struck him in the chest. He turned away from me, took one step and fell. I sent another arrow toward him which went wide.

At this time three more dogs trotted out of the cave. I used the last of my arrows and killed two of them.

Carrying both of the spears, I climbed down from the ledge and went through the brush to the place where the leader had fallen. He was not there. While I had been shooting at the other dogs, he had gone. He could not have gone far because of his wound, but though I looked everywhere, around the ledge where I had been standing and in front of the cave, I did not find him.

I waited for a long time and then went inside the cave. It was deep, but I could see clearly.

Far back in a corner was the half-eaten carcass of a fox. Beside it was a black dog with four gray pups.

One of the pups came slowly toward me, a round ball of fur that I could have held in my hand. I wanted to hold it, but the mother leaped to her feet and bared her teeth. I raised my spear as I backed out of the cave, yet I did not use it. The wounded leader was not there.

Night was coming and I left the cave, going along the foot of the hill that led to the cliff. I had not gone far on this trail that the wild dogs used when I saw the broken shaft of an arrow. It had been gnawed off near the tip and I knew it was from the arrow which had wounded the leader.

Farther on I saw his tracks in the dust. They were uneven as if he were traveling slowly. I followed them toward the cliff, but finally lost them in the darkness.

The next day and the next it rained and I did not go to look for him. I spent those days making more arrows, and on the third day, with these arrows and my spear, I went out along the trail the wild dogs had made to and from my house.

There were no tracks after the rain, but I followed the trail to the pile of rocks where I had seen them before. On the far side of the rocks I found the big gray dog. He had the broken arrow in his chest and he was lying with one of his legs under him.

He was about ten paces from me so I could see

him clearly. I was sure that he was dead, but I lifted the spear and took good aim at him. Just as I was about to throw the spear, he raised his head a little from the earth and then let it drop.

This surprised me greatly and I stood there for a while not knowing what to do, whether to use the spear or my bow. I was used to animals playing dead until they suddenly turned on you or ran away.

The spear was the better of the two weapons at this distance, but I could not use it as well as the other, so I climbed onto the rocks where I could see him if he ran. I placed my feet carefully. I had a second arrow ready should I need it. I fitted an arrow and pulled back the string, aiming at his head.

Why I did not send the arrow I cannot say. I stood on the rock with the bow pulled back and my hand would not let it go. The big dog lay there and did not move and this may be the reason. If he had gotten up I would have killed him. I stood there for a long time looking down at him and then I climbed off the rocks.

He did not move when I went up to him, nor could I see him breathing until I was very close. The head of the arrow was in his chest and the broken shaft was covered with blood. The thick fur around his neck was matted from the rain.

I do not think that he knew I was picking him up, for his body was limp, as if he were dead. He was very heavy and the only way I could lift him was by kneeling and putting his legs around my shoulders.

In this manner, stopping to rest when I was tired, I carried him to the headland.

I could not get through the opening under the fence, so I cut the bindings and lifted out two of the whale ribs and thus took him into the house. He did not look at me or raise his head when I laid him on the floor, but his mouth was open and he was breathing.

The arrow had a small point, which was fortunate, and came out easily though it had gone deep. He did not move while I did this, nor afterwards as I cleaned the wound with a peeled stick from a coral bush. This bush has poisonous berries, yet its wood often heals wounds that nothing else will.

I had not gathered food for many days and the baskets were empty, so I left water for the dog and, after mending the fence, went down to the sea. I had no thought that he would live and I did not care.

All day I was among the rocks gathering shellfish and only once did I think of the wounded dog, my enemy, lying there in the house, and then to wonder why I had not killed him.

He was still alive when I got back, though he had not moved from the place where I had left him. Again I cleaned the wound with a coral twig. I then lifted his head and put water in his mouth, which he swallowed. This was the first time that he had looked at me since the time I had found him on the trail. His eyes were sunken and they looked out at me from far back in his head.

Before I went to sleep I gave him more water. In the morning I left food for him when I went down to the sea, and when I came home he had eaten it. He was lying in the corner, watching me. While I made a fire and cooked my supper, he watched me. His yellow eyes followed me wherever I moved.

That night I slept on the rock, for I was afraid of him, and at dawn as I went out I left the hole under the fence open so he could go. But he was there when I got back, lying in the sun with his head on his paws. I had speared two fish, which I cooked for my supper. Since he was very thin, I gave him one of them, and after he had eaten it he came over and lay down by the fire, watching me with his yellow eyes that were very narrow and slanted up at the corners.

Four nights I slept on the rock, and every morning I left the hole under the fence open so he could leave. Each day I speared a fish for him and when I got home he was always at the fence waiting for it. He would not take the fish from me so I had to put it on the ground. Once I held out my hand to him, but at this he backed away and showed his teeth.

On the fourth day when I came back from the rocks early he was not there at the fence waiting. A strange feeling came over me. Always before when I returned, I had hoped that he would be gone. But now as I crawled under the fence I did not feel the same.

I called out, "Dog, Dog," for I had no other name for him.

I ran toward the house, calling it. He was inside. He was just getting to his feet, stretching himself and yawning. He looked first at the fish I carried and then at me and moved his tail.

That night I stayed in the house. Before I fell asleep I thought of a name for him, for I could not call him Dog. The name I thought of was Rontu, which means in our language Fox Eyes.

16

THE WHITE MEN's ship did not return that spring or in the summer. But every day, whether I was on the headland or gathering shellfish on the rocks or working on my canoe, I watched for it. I also watched for the red ship of the Aleuts.

I was not sure what I would do if the Aleuts came. I could hide in the cave which I had stored with food and water, for it was surrounded by thick brush and the mouth of the ravine could only be reached from the sea. The Aleuts had not used the spring and did not know about it because there was another one closer to where they had camped. But they might come upon the cave by chance and then I must be ready to flee.

For this reason I worked on the canoe I had abandoned on the spit. I went to the place where the others were hidden, but they were dried out and cracked. Also they were too heavy for a girl to push into the water, even a girl as strong as I was.

The tides had almost buried the canoe, and I labored many days to dig it out of the sand. Since the weather was warm, I did not go back and forth to my house on the headland, but cooked my meals on the sandspit and at night slept in the canoe, which saved much time.

Even this canoe was too big for me to pull easily in and out of the water, so I set about making it smaller. I did this by loosening all the planks, by cutting the sinews and heating the pitch that bound them together. I then shaped these planks to half their length, using sharp knives made from a black stone which is to be found at one place on the island, and bound them back together with fresh pitch and sinews.

The canoe when I had finished was not so beautiful as it had been before, but I could now lift one end of it and drag it through the waves.

All the time I was working on the canoe, which was most of that summer, Rontu was with me. He was either sleeping in the shade of the canoe or running up and down the sandspit chasing the pelicans that roost there in great numbers because there are numerous fish nearby. He never caught any of the birds, yet he would keep trying until his tongue hung out of his mouth.

He had learned his name quickly and many

words that meant something to him. *Zalwit,* for example, which is our word for pelican, and *naip* which means fish. I talked to him often, using these words and others and many that he did not understand, just as though I were talking to one of my people.

"Rontu," I would say after he had stolen a special fish I had speared for my supper, "tell me why it is that you are such a handsome dog and yet such a thief."

He would put his head on one side and then the other, although he knew only two of the words, and look at me.

Or I would say, "It is a beautiful day. I have never seen the ocean so calm and the sky looks like a blue shell. How long do you think these days will last?"

Rontu would look up at me just the same, though he understood none of the words, acting as if he did.

Because of this I was not lonely. I did not know how lonely I had been until I had Rontu to talk to.

When the canoe was finished and the pitch had dried I wanted to find out how it went through the water and if the planks leaked, so we set off on a long voyage around the island. The voyage took all of one day, from dawn until night.

There are many sea caves on the Island of the Blue Dolphins and some of them are large and go far back into the cliffs. One of these was near the headland where my house stood.

The opening was narrow, not much wider than the canoe, but once we were inside, it spread out and was larger than my place on the headland.

The walls were black and smooth and slanted far up over my head. The water was almost as black, except where light came through the opening. Here it was a gold color and you could see fish swimming around. They were different from the fish on the reefs, having larger eyes and fins that drifted out from their bodies like kelp.

This place opened into another, which was smaller and so dark I could see nothing. It was very silent in there, with no sound of the waves on the shore and only the lapping of the water against the rocky walls. I thought of the god Tumaiyowit who had become angry at Mukat and gone down, down into another world, and I wondered if it were not to such a place as this that he had gone.

Far ahead was a spot of light no larger than my hand, so instead of turning back, which I felt like doing, I drifted toward it around many turnings and came at last to another room much like the first.

Along one side was a wide shelf of rock, which ran out to the sea through a narrow opening. The tide was full and yet the shelf was out of the water. It was a fine place to hide a canoe, which could be lifted out and stored there where no one could find it. The ledge joined the cliff just below my house. All I needed was a trail down to the cave and then the canoe would be close at hand.

"We have made a great discovery," I said to Rontu.

Rontu did not hear me. He was watching a devil-fish, just beyond the opening of the cave. This fish has a small head with eyes that bulge and many arms. All day Rontu had been barking — at the cormorants, the gulls, the seals — at everything that moved. Now he was quiet, watching the black thing in the water.

I let the canoe drift along and knelt down out of sight until I could pick up my spear.

The devilfish was in front of us, swimming slowly near the surface, moving all his arms at once. Large devilfish are dangerous if you are in the sea, for their arms are as long as a man, and they can quickly wrap them around you. They also have a big mouth and a sharp beak where their arms join their head. This one was the largest I had ever seen.

Since Rontu was standing in front of me and I could not put the canoe into a better position, I had to lean out to use the spear. As I did so, the devil-fish saw my movement and let loose in the water a black cloud of liquid which instantly hid him from view.

I knew that the devilfish would not be in the center of this cloud, that he had left it behind. I therefore did not aim my spear at it, but picked up the paddle and waited until he appeared. He was now twice the length of the canoe from me and though I paddled fast I could not overtake him.

"Rontu," I said, for he was watching the black cloud in the water, "you have much to learn about the devilfish."

Rontu did not look at me or bark. He put his head to one side and then the other, still puzzled, more so when the cloud disappeared and nothing was left except clear water.

Devilfish is the best food in the seas. The flesh is white and tender and very sweet. But they are difficult to catch without a special kind of spear, which I now decided to make during the winter when I would have much time.

I took the canoe to Coral Cove, not far from the cave, and pulled it up on the shore out of reach of the winter storms. There it would be safe until spring when I would hide it in the cave that Rontu and I had found. It was easy to paddle and did not leak. I was very happy.

17

Storms came early with rain and between the rains fierce winds struck the island and filled the air with sand. During this time, I made myself another dress, but most of the days I spent fashioning a spear to catch the giant devilfish.

I had seen this spear made, as I had seen my father make bows and arrows, yet I knew little about it, no more than I had about the others. Still I remembered how it looked and how it was used. From these memories I made it after many errors and many hours of work, sitting on the floor while Rontu slept nearby and the storms beat upon the roof.

Four of the sea-elephant teeth were left, and though I broke all except one, this I worked down to a head with a barbed point. I then made a ring and fastened it to the end of the shaft, and into this ring fitted the head, which was tied to a long string made of braided sinew. When the spear was thrown and struck a devilfish, the head came loose from the shaft. The shaft floated on the water, but the pointed barb was held by the string which was tied to your wrist. This spear was especially good because it could be thrown from a distance.

On the first day of spring I went down to Coral Cove with my new spear. I knew it was spring because that morning at dawn the sky was filled with flocks of darting birds. They were small and black and came only at this time of year. They came out of the south and stayed for two suns, hunting food in the ravines, and then flew off in one great flight toward the north.

Rontu did not go with me to the beach because I had let him out of the fence and he had not returned. The wild dogs had been to the house many times that winter and he had paid no heed to them, but the night before, after they had come and gone, he had stood at the fence. He stood and whined and walked up and down. It worried me to see him act so strangely, and when he refused to eat I finally let him out.

Now I pushed the canoe into the water and drifted toward the reef where the devilfish lived. The water was so clear that it was like the air around me. Far down, the sea ferns moved as though a breeze were blowing there, and among them swam the devilfish trailing their long arms.

It was good to be on the sea after the winter storms, with the new spear in my hand, but all the morning as I hunted the giant devilfish I kept thinking of Rontu. I should have been happy, yet thinking of him I was not. Would he come back, I wondered, or had he gone to live with the wild dogs? Would he again be my enemy? If he were my enemy, I knew that I could never kill him, now that he had been my friend.

When the sun was high I hid the canoe in the cave we had found, for once more it was the time the Aleuts might return, and with the two small bass I had speared, though not the giant devilfish, I went up the cliff. I had planned to make a trail from the cave to my house, but had decided that it could be seen from a ship and by anyone standing on the headland.

The climb was steep. As I reached the top, I paused for breath. The morning was quiet except for the noise of the little birds flying from bush to bush and the cries of the gulls who did not like these strangers. Then I heard the sound of dogs fighting. The sound came from far off, perhaps from the ravine, and taking my bow and arrows, I hurried in that direction.

I went down the path which led to the spring. There were tracks of the wild dogs around the spring, and among them I saw the large ones of Rontu. The tracks led away through the ravine which winds to the sea. I heard again the distant sound of fighting.

I went slowly through the ravine because of my bow and arrows.

At last I came to the place where it opens into a meadow right at the edge of a low sea cliff. Sometimes in the summers, a long time ago, my people had lived here. They gathered shellfish on the rocks and ate them here, leaving the shells which after many summers had formed a mound. Over this grass had grown, and a thick-leaved plant called *gnapan*.

On this mound, among the grasses and the plants, stood Rontu. He stood facing me, with his back to the sea cliff. In front of him in a half-circle were the wild dogs. At first I thought that the pack had driven him there against the cliff and were getting ready to attack him. But I soon saw that two dogs stood out from the rest of the pack, between it and Rontu, and that their muzzles were wet with blood.

One of these dogs was the leader who had taken Rontu's place when he had come to live with me. The other one, which was spotted, I had never seen. The battle was between Rontu and these two dogs. The rest were there to fall upon whichever was beaten.

So great was the noise made by the pack, they had not heard me as I came through the brush, nor did they see me now as I stood at the edge of the meadow. They sat on their haunches and barked, with their eyes fixed on the others. But I was sure that Rontu knew I was somewhere near, for he raised his head and smelled the air.

The two dogs were trotting back and forth along the foot of the mound, watching Rontu. The fight had probably started at the spring and they had stalked him to this place where he had chosen to fight.

The sea cliff was behind him and they could not reach him from that direction so they were trying to think of some other way. It would have been easier if one could have attacked him from the back and one from the front.

Rontu did not move from where he stood on top of the mound. Now and again he lowered his head to lick a wound on his leg, but whenever he did he always kept his eyes on the two dogs trotting up and down.

I could have shot them, for they were within reach of my bow, or driven off the pack, yet I stood in the brush and watched. This was a battle between them and Rontu. If I stopped it, they would surely fight again, perhaps at some other place less favorable to him.

Rontu again licked his wound and this time he did not watch the two dogs moving slowly past the mound. I thought it was a lure and so it proved to be, for suddenly they ran toward him. They came from opposite sides of the mound, ears laid back and teeth bared.

Rontu did not wait for the attack, but, leaping at the nearer one, turned his shoulder and with his head lowered caught the dog's foreleg. The pack was quiet. In the silence, I could hear the sound of the bone breaking, and the dog backed away on three legs.

The spotted dog had reached the top of the mound. Whirling away from the one he had crippled, Rontu faced him, but not in time to fend off the first heavy rush. Teeth slashed at his throat and, as he turned his body, struck him instead on the flank, and he went down.

At that moment, while he lay there on the grass with the dog circling warily and the pack moving slowly toward him, without knowing that I did so, I fitted an arrow to the bow. A good distance separated Rontu from his attacker and I could end the battle before he was wounded further or the pack fell upon him. Yet, as before, I did not send the arrow.

The spotted dog paused, and turned in his tracks, and again leaped, this time from behind.

Rontu was still lying in the grass with his paws under him and I thought he did not see that the other was upon him. But crouching there, he suddenly raised himself and at the same time fastened his teeth in the dog's throat.

Together they rolled off the mound, yet Rontu did not let go. The pack sat restless in the grass.

In a short time Rontu rose to his feet and left the spotted dog where it lay. He walked to the top of the mound and lifted his head and gave a long howl. I had never heard this sound before. It was the sound of many things that I did not understand.

He trotted past me and up the ravine. When I got to the house he was there waiting, as if he had not been away or nothing had happened.

In all the time he lived, Rontu never left again, and the wild dogs, which for some reason divided into two packs, after that never returned to the headland.

18

Flowers were plentiful that spring because of the winter's heavy rains. The dunes were covered with mats of sand flowers, which are red and have tiny eyes that are sometimes pink and sometimes white. Yuccas grew tall among the rocks of the ravine. Their heads were clustered with curly globes no larger than pebbles and the color of the sun when it rises. Lupines grew where the springs ran. From the sunny cliffs, in crevices where no one would think anything could grow, sprang the little red and yellow fountains of the comul bush.

Birds were plentiful, too. There were many hummers which can stand still in the air and look like bits of polished stone and have long tongues to sip honey with. There were blue jays, which are very quarrelsome birds, and black-and-white peckers that pecked holes in the yucca stalks and the poles of my roof, even in the whale bones of the fence. Red-winged blackbirds also came flying out of the south, and flocks of crows, and a bird with a yellow body and a scarlet head, which I had never seen before.

A pair of these birds made a nest in a stunted tree near my house. It was made from strings of the yucca bush and had a small opening at the top and hung down like a pouch. The mother laid two speckled eggs which she and her mate took turns sitting on. After the eggs hatched, I put shreds of abalone under the tree and these she fed her young.

The young birds were not like their mother and father, being gray and very ugly, but anyway, I took them from the nest and put them in a small cage that I made of reeds. So later in the spring, when all the birds except the crows left the island and flew off to the north, I had these two for friends.

They soon grew beautiful feathers like those of their parents and began to make the same sound, which was *reep, reep*. But it was soft and clear and much sweeter than the cries of the gulls or the crows or the talk of the pelicans which sounds like the quarreling of toothless old men.

Before summer came the cage was too small for my two birds, but instead of building a larger one, I cut the tips of their wings, one wing of each, so they could not fly away, and let them loose in the house. By the time their wings had grown out, they had learned to take food from my hand. They would jump down from the roof and perch on my arm and beg, making their *reep, reep* sound.

When their wings began to feather out, I cut them again. This time I let them loose in the yard, where they hopped around hunting food, perching on Rontu who by now had gotten used to them. The next time they feathered out, I did not trim their wings, but they never flew farther away than the ravine and would always come back at night to sleep and, no matter how much they had eaten, to ask for food.

One, because he was larger, I called Tainor. I named him after a young man I liked who had been killed by the Aleuts. The other was called Lurai, which was a name I wished I had been called instead of Karana.

During the time that I was taming the birds, I made another skirt. This one I also made of yucca fibers softened in water and braided into twine. I made it just like the others, with folds running lengthwise. It was open on both sides and hung to my knees. The belt I made of sealskin which could be tied in a knot. I also made a pair of sandals from sealskin for walking over the dunes when the sun was hot, or just to be dressed up when I wore my new skirt of yucca twine.

Often I would put on the skirt and the sandals

and walk along the cliff with Rontu. Sometimes I made a wreath of flowers and fastened it in my hair. After the Aleuts had killed our men at Coral Cove, all the women of our tribe had singed their hair short as a sign of mourning. I had singed mine, too, with a faggot, but now it had grown long again and came to my waist. I parted it and let it fall down my back, except when I wore a wreath. Then I made braids and fastened them with long whale-bone pins.

I also made a wreath for Rontu's neck, which he did not like. Together we would walk along the cliff looking at the sea, and though the white men's ship did not return that spring, it was a happy time. The air smelled of flowers and birds sang everywhere.

19

Another summer had come and still I had not speared the giant devilfish that lived near the cave.

Every day during the spring, Rontu and I went to look for him. I would put the canoe in the water and paddle slowly through the cave, from one opening to the other, often several times. I saw many devilfish there where the black water is streaked with light, but not the giant one.

At last I gave up looking for him and began to gather abalones for winter. The red shells hold the sweetest meat and are best for drying, though the green ones and the black are also good. Because the red ones are the sweetest, starfish prey upon them.

This star-shaped creature places itself over the shell of an abalone. With its five arms spread out against the rock to which the abalone is fastened, it holds the shell with its suckers, and then begins to lift itself. The starfish pulls against the abalone shell, sometimes for days, holding on with its suckers and pushing up with its legs, until little by little the heavy shell comes loose from the body.

One morning we left the cave and paddled out to the reef which is joined to it.

For many days I had been gathering a few shellfish on the rocks at Coral Cove, but I had been watching the reef and waiting for the right time to harvest. This is when there are few starfish feeding, for they are as hard to pry loose from an abalone as an abalone is to pry from a rock.

The tide was low and the reef rose far out of the water. Along its sides were great numbers of red abalones and very few starfish, so before the sun was high I filled the bottom of the canoe.

The day was windless, and since I had all I could carry, I tied the canoe, and with Rontu following me, climbed onto the reef to look for fish to spear for our supper.

Blue dolphins were leaping beyond the kelp beds. In the kelp otter were playing at the games they never tire of. And around me everywhere the gulls were fishing for scallops, which were numerous that summer. They grow on the floating kelp leaves and there were so many of them that much of the kelp near the reef had been dragged to the bottom. Still there were scallops that the gulls could reach, and taking them in their beaks they would fly far above the reef and let them drop. The gulls would then swoop down to the rocks and pick the meat from the broken shells.

Scallops fell on the reef like rain, which amused me, but not Rontu who could not understand what the gulls were doing. Dodging this way and that I went to the end of the reef where the biggest fish live. With a sinew line and a hook made of abalone shell I caught two that had large heads and long teeth, but are good to eat. I gave one to Rontu and on the way back to the canoe gathered purple sea urchins to use for dyeing.

Rontu, who was trotting along in front of me, suddenly dropped his fish and stood looking down over the edge of the reef.

There, swimming in the clear water, was a devilfish. It was the same one I had been hunting for. It was the giant!

Seldom did you see any devilfish here, for they like deep places, and the water along this part of the reef is shallow. Perhaps this one lived in the cave and came here only when he could not find food.

Rontu made no sound. I fixed the head of the spear and the long string that held it to my wrist. I then crawled back to the edge of the reef.

The giant had not moved. He was floating just below the surface of the water and I could plainly see his eyes. They were the size of small stones and stood out from his head, with black rims and gold centers and in the centers a black spot, like the eyes of a spirit I had once seen on a night that rain fell and lightning forked in the sky.

Where my hands rested was a deep crevice and in it a fish was hiding.

The giant was half the length of my spear from the reef, but while I watched, one of his long arms ran out like a snake and felt its way into the crevice. It went past the fish and along the side of the rock and then the end of it curled back. As the arm gently wound itself around the fish from behind, I rose to one knee and drove the spear.

I aimed at the giant's head, but though it was larger than my two fishes and a good target, I missed. The spear struck down through the water and slanted off. Instantly a black cloud surrounded the devilfish. The only thing I could see of him was one long arm still grasping his prey.

I jumped to my feet to pull in the spear, thinking that I might have a chance to throw it again. As I did so, the shaft bobbed back to the surface and I saw that the barbed point had come loose.

At the same moment the string tightened. My grip on it broke, and aware that I had struck the devilfish, I quickly dropped the coils I held, for when the string runs out fast it burns your hands or becomes entangled.

The devilfish does not swim with fins or flippers, like other things in the sea. He takes water in through the hole in the front of his body and pushes the water out behind through two slits. When he is swimming slowly you can see these two streams trailing out, but only then. When he moves fast, you can see nothing except a streak in the water.

The coils I had dropped on the rock hopped and sang as they ran. Then there were no more of them. The string tightened on my wrist and, to lessen the shock, I leaped across the crevice in the direction the giant had taken. With the string in both hands, but still fastened to my wrist, I braced my feet on the slippery rock and leaned backwards.

The string snapped tight with the weight of the devilfish. It began to stretch, and fearing that it might break, I walked forward, yet I made him pull me every step.

He was moving toward the cave, along the edge of the reef. The cave was a good distance away. If he got there I would surely lose him. The canoe was tied just in front of me. Once I was in it, I could let him pull me until he grew tired. But there was no way to untie the canoe and still hold on to the string.

Rontu all this time was running up and down the

reef barking and leaping at me, which made my task harder.

Step by step I walked forward, until the devilfish was in the deep water close to the cave. He was so close that I had to stop, even if the sinew broke and I lost him. I therefore braced myself and did not move. The sinew stretched, throwing off drops of water. I could hear it stretch and I was sure it would break. I did not feel it cutting into my hands, though they bled.

The pull suddenly lessened and I was sure that he was gone, but the next instant I saw the string cutting the water in a wide circle. He was swimming off from the cave and the reef toward some rocks that were about twice the length of the string away. He would be safe there, too, for among them were many places to hide.

I pulled in half the string while he was moving toward the rocks, but soon had to let it out It grew tight and again began to stretch. The water here was only a little over my waist, and I let myself down over the reef.

There was a sand bar not far from the rocks, and stepping carefully on the bottom, which was full of holes, I slowly made my way toward it. Rontu swam along by my side.

I reached the sand bar before the devilfish could hide himself in the rocks. The string held and he turned about and once more swam toward the cave. Twice again he did this. Each time I took in some of the string. The third time, as he came up into the shallow water, I walked backward across the sand bar so he would not see me, and pulled on the string with all my strength.

The giant slid up on the sand. He lay with his arms spread out, partly in the water, and I thought he was dead. Then I saw his eyes moving. Before I could shout a warning, Rontu had rushed forward and seized him. But the devilfish was too heavy to lift or shake. As Rontu's jaws sought another hold, three of the many arms wound themselves around his neck.

Devilfish are only dangerous when in the water where they can fasten themselves to you with their long arms. These arms have rows of suckers underneath them and they can drag you under and hold you there until you drown. But even on land the devilfish can injure you, for he is strong and does not die quickly.

The giant was flailing his arms, struggling to get back into the water. Little by little he was dragging Rontu with him. I could no longer use the string because it was wound around Rontu's legs.

The whalebone knife I used for prying abalones from the rocks was tied to a thong at my waist. The blade was thick at the point but had a sharp edge. I dropped the coils of string and unfastened the knife as I ran.

I ran past the devilfish and got between him and the deep water. So many of his arms were flailing that it was useless to cut any one of them. One struck me on the leg and burned like a whip. Another, which Rontu had chewed off, lay wriggling at the edge of the water, as if it were looking for something to fasten on to.

The head rose out of the twisting arms like a giant stalk. The gold eyes with their black rims were fixed on me. Above the sounds of the waves and the water splashing and Rontu's barking, I could hear the snapping of his beak, which was sharper than the knife I held in my hand.

I drove the knife down into his body and as I did this I was suddenly covered, or so it seemed, with a countless number of leeches, sucking at my skin. Fortunately one hand was free, the hand that held the knife, and again and again I struck down through the tough hide. The suckers, which were fastened to me and pained greatly, lessened their hold. Slowly the arms stopped moving and then grew limp.

I tried to drag the devilfish out of the water, but my strength was gone. I did not even go back to the reef for my canoe, though I did take the shaft and the head of the spear, which had cost me much labor, and the sinew line.

It was night before Rontu and I got back to the house.

Rontu had a gash on his nose from the giant's beak, and I had many cuts and bruises. I saw two more giant devilfish along the reef that summer, but I did not try to spear them.

20

I GATHERED two more canoeloads of abalones soon after that, mostly the sweet red ones, which I cleaned and carried to the house. Along the south part of the fence where the sun shone most of the day, I built long shelves out of branches and put the meat up to dry. Abalones are larger than your hand and twice as thick when fresh, but they shrink small in the sun so you have to dry many.

In the old days on the island there were children to keep away the gulls, which would rather feast on abalones than anything else. In one morning, if the meat was left unguarded, they could fly off with a month's harvest.

At first, whenever I went to the spring or to the beach, I left Rontu behind to chase them off, but he did not like this and howled all the time I was gone. Finally I tied strings to some of the abalone shells and hung them from poles. The insides of the shells are bright and catch the sun and they turn one way and another in the wind. After that I had little trouble with the gulls.

I also caught small fish in a net I had made and hung them up to dry for winter light. With meat drying on the shelves and the shells flashing and turning in the wind and the strings of fish hanging on the fence, the yard looked as if a whole village were living there on the headland instead of just Rontu and me.

Every morning after I had gathered food for winter, we went out on the sea. At the end of summer I would gather roots and seeds to store, but now there was nothing that needed to be done. We went many places those first days of summer — to the beach where the sea elephants lived, to Black Cave which was even larger than the first cave we found, and to Tall Rock where the cormorants roosted.

Tall Rock was more than a league from the island and was black and shimmering because it was covered with cormorants. I killed ten of the birds the first time we went there and I skinned and fleshed them and put them out to dry, for someday I wanted to make myself a skirt of cormorant feathers.

Black Cave was on the south coast of the island, near the place where the canoes were stored. In front of the cave was a high ledge of rocks surrounded by deep kelp beds, and I would have paddled by it if I had not seen a sea hawk fly out. The sun was in the west and I had a long way to go to reach home, but I was curious about the hawk and the place he lived in.

The opening of the cave was small, like the one in the cave under the headland, and Rontu and I had to crouch low to get through. Weak light came from outside and I saw that we were in a room with black, shining walls that curved high overhead. At the far end of the room was another small opening. It was long and very dark, but when we reached the end of it we were in another room which was larger than the first and lit with a shaft of light. The light came from the sun, which shone down through a jagged crack in the ceiling.

Seeing the sun shining down and the black shadows drifting over the walls, Rontu barked, then began to howl. The sound echoed through the cave like the howling of a whole pack of dogs. It sent a cold feeling down my back.

"Be quiet!" I shouted, putting my hand over his jaws. My words echoed and echoed in the room.

I turned the canoe around and started back toward the opening. Above it, on a deep ledge that ran from one side of the room to the other, my gaze fell upon a row of strange figures. There must have been two dozen of them standing against the black wall. They were as tall as I, with long arms and legs and short bodies made of reeds and clothed in gull feathers. Each one had eyes fashioned of round or oblong disks of abalone shell, but the rest of their faces were blank. The eyes glittered down at me, moved as the light on the water moved and was reflected upon them. They were more alive than the eyes of those who live.

In the middle of the group was a seated figure, a skeleton. It sat leaning against the wall with its knees drawn up and in its fingers, which were raised to its mouth, a flute of pelican bone.

There were other things there on the ledge, in the shadows among the standing figures, but having drifted far back in the room, I again paddled toward the opening. I had forgotten that the tide was coming in. To my great surprise the opening had narrowed. It was too small now for me to get through. We would have to stay there in the room until the tide went out, until dawn came.

I paddled to the far end of the cave. I did not look back at the glittering eyes of the figures on the ledge. I crouched in the bottom of the canoe and watched the shaft of light grow weak. The opening out to the sea grew smaller and finally disappeared. Night came and a star showed through the crevice overhead.

This star passed out of sight and another took its place. The tide lifted the canoe higher in the room, and as the water lapped against the walls it sounded like the soft music of a flute. It played many tunes through the long night and I slept little, watching the stars change. I knew that the skeleton who sat on the ledge playing his flute was one of my ancestors, and the others with the glittering eyes, though only images, were too, but still I was sleepless and afraid.

With the first light, another high tide almost setting, we left the cave. I did not look up at those standing quietly on the ledge or at the flute player playing for them, but paddled fast out into the morning sea. Nor did I look back.

"I suppose this cave once had a name," I said to Rontu, who was as glad to be free as I was, "but I have never heard of it or heard it spoken about. We will call it Black Cave and never in all our days go there again."

When we came back from our voyage to Tall Rock, I hid the canoe in the cave below the headland. It was hard work, but each time I would lift the canoe from the water and onto the ledge, even though I planned to go out the next morning.

Two summers had come and gone and the Aleut hunters had not returned, yet during these days I always looked for them. At dawn, as Rontu and I went down the cliff, I would watch the ocean for their sails. The summer air was clear and I could see many leagues. Wherever we went in the canoe I would never be gone longer than half a day. On the way home, I always paddled close to shore and looked for them.

It was the last time that we went to Tall Rock that the Aleuts came.

I had hidden the canoe and climbed the cliff with the ten cormorant skins slung over my back. At the top of the cliff I stood for a while gazing at the sea. There were some small clouds on the water. One of them, the smallest, did not look like the others and as I watched, I saw that it was a ship.

The sun made bright scales on the water, but I could see clearly. There were two sails and it was a ship coming toward the island. For a long time I could not tell the color of the sails. I wondered if it could be the white men, though now I thought about them little and seldom looked for them.

I left the cormorants hanging on the fence and went to the rock on the headland. I could see no better from the rock because the sun was low and the whole ocean was covered with light. Then as I stood there I remembered that the white men's ship would come from the east. This one had came from a different direction — from the north.

I still was not sure that it belonged to the Aleuts, but I decided to pack the things that I would take to the cave in the ravine. There was much to take —

my two birds, the skirt I had made, the stone utensils, my beads and earrings, the cormorant feathers, and all of my baskets and weapons. The abalones were not yet dry so I would have to leave them.

When I had packed everything and put it beside the hole under the fence, I went back to the headland. I lay on the rock so I would not be seen and peered over its rim toward the north. For a moment I did not find the ship, and then I saw that it had traveled faster than I thought it would. It was already rounding the kelp bed, close to the rocks of Coral Cove. The last of the sun shone on the ship, on the bow, which was made like the beak of a bird, and on the two red sails.

I knew that the Aleuts would not come on shore in the dark, and that I had until morning to carry my things to the cave, but I did not wait. Most of the night I worked, making two trips to the cave. At dawn, when everything had been moved, I went back to the house for the last time. There I buried the ashes of my fires and threw sand over the shelves and the floor. I took down the shells I had put up to scare the gulls and tossed them and the abalones over the cliff. At last, with a pelican wing, I brushed away the marks of my feet. When I had finished, it looked as though no one had lived there for a long time.

By now the sun was up and I climbed onto the

rock. The ship lay at anchor in the cove. Canoes were bringing goods to the shore and some were out in the kelp beds, beginning to hunt for otter. There was a fire on the shore and beside it, a girl. She was cooking something and I could see the fire shining on her hair.

I did not stay long on the headland. Always in the past I had gone to the ravine by a different way so as not to wear a trail. This time I went off toward the west, along the cliff, and then doubled back through the brush, being careful to leave no tracks. Rontu's prints did not matter because the Aleuts knew that there were dogs on the island.

The cave was very dark and I had trouble getting Rontu to go through the small opening. Only after I had crawled in and out several times would he follow me. I closed the opening with stones, and since I was tired, lay down and slept all that day. I slept until I could see the stars shining between the cracks in the rocks.

21

I DID NOT take Rontu with me when I left the cave that night. And I closed the opening so that he would not follow me, for if the Aleuts had brought their dogs, he would surely smell them out. I went quietly through the brush to the headland.

Before I had climbed to the top of the high rock I could see the glow of the Aleut fires. They had camped on the mesa, at the place and the spring they had used before. It was less than half a league from my cave.

I stood for a long time watching the fires, wondering if I should move to another part of the island, perhaps to the cave where the wild dogs had lived. I was not afraid that the men would discover me, because they worked on the beach or hunted in their canoes all day. It was the girl I was afraid of. The ravine was tangled with brush, which was hard to walk through, but in the ravine grew seeds and roots. Sometime when she was out looking for food she might wander by the spring and see that it was being used and find my steps leading to the cave.

I stood on the rock until the Aleut fires died. I thought of everything I could do, of the different places I could go, and at last decided to stay in the ravine. The far end of the island had no springs, and if I moved there I would have no place to hide the canoe which I might need.

I went back to the cave and did not leave it until the moon was full. There was little food left. Rontu and I climbed to the headland and when we passed the house I saw that three of the whale ribs had been cut from the fence. No one was there or else Rontu would have barked. I waited until the tide was low, which was close to dawn, and filled a basket with sea water and abalones. We were back in the cave before it grew light.

The sea water kept the abalones fresh, but when we had to go out again the night was too dark to find our way to the reef. I therefore had to gather roots. I could never gather many before the sun rose, so I went out every morning until the next moon came. Then I went to the reef for abalones.

During all this time I saw none of the Aleuts. Nor did the girl come near the cave, though I found her footsteps far down the ravine where she had been to dig roots. The Aleuts had not brought their dogs, which was fortunate, for they would have found Rontu's tracks and followed us to the cave.

The days were long for Rontu and me. At first he would pace up and down the cave and stand at the opening sniffing through the cracks. I did not let him out except when I was with him for fear he would go to the camp and not come back. After a while he got used to this and would lie all day and watch whatever I was doing.

It was dark in the cave, even when the sun was high, so I burned the small fish I had stored. By their light I began to make a cormorant skirt, working every day on it. The ten skins I had taken at Tall Rock were now dry and in condition to sew. All of them were from male cormorants whose feathers are thicker than those of the females and much glossier. The skirt of yucca fibers was simple to make. I wanted this one to be better, so I cut the skins carefully and sewed them with great care.

I made the bottom first, putting the skins end to end, and using three of them. For the rest of the skirt I sewed the others along their sides so that the feathers ran one way on the upper part and a different way along the bottom.

It was a beautiful skirt and I finished it on the day after the second moon. I had burned all of the little fish, and since I could catch no more until the

Aleuts left, I took the skirt outside to work on it there. I had found footsteps in the ravine twice again after the first time, but no closer to the cave. I had begun to feel safe, for the winter storms would soon be here and the Aleuts would leave. Before another moon they would be gone.

I had never seen the skirt in the sunlight. It was black, but underneath were green and gold colors, and all the feathers shimmered as though they were on fire. It was more beautiful than I had thought it would be. I worked fast now that it was almost finished, yet from time to time I would stop to hold it against my waist.

"Rontu," I said, feeling giddy with happiness, "if you were not a male dog I would make you one too, as beautiful as this."

Rontu, who was sprawled out at the mouth of the cave, raised his head and yawned at me and went back to sleep.

I was standing in the sunlight, holding the skirt to my waist, when Rontu leaped to his feet. I heard the sound of steps. It came from the direction of the spring and as I turned quickly I saw a girl looking down at me from the brush.

My spear stood beside the mouth of the cave within easy reach. The girl was not more than ten paces from me and with one movement I could have picked up the spear and thrown it. Why I did not throw the spear, I do not know, for she was one of the Aleuts who had killed my people on the beach of Coral Cove.

She said something and Rontu left the mouth of the cave and walked slowly toward her. The hair raised on his neck, but then he walked to where she stood and let her touch him.

The girl looked at me and made a motion with her hands which I took to mean that Rontu was hers.

"No," I cried and shook my head.

I picked up my spear.

She started to turn and I thought that she was going to flee back through the brush. She made another motion which I took to mean that Rontu was now mine. I did not believe her. I held the spear over my shoulder, ready to throw.

"Tutok," she said, pointing to herself.

I did not say my name. I called Rontu and he came back.

The girl looked at him and then at me and smiled. She was older than I, but not so tall. She had a broad face and small eyes that were very black. When she smiled, I saw that her teeth were worn down from chewing seal sinew, but they were very white.

I was still holding the cormorant skirt and the girl pointed to it and said something. There was one word — *wintscha* — which sounded like a word that means pretty in our language.

I was so proud of the skirt that I did not think. The spear was in my hand, but I held up the skirt so the sunlight could shine on all of it.

The girl jumped down from the ledge and came over to me and touched it.

"*Wintscha*," she said again.

I did not say the word, but she wanted to hold the skirt and I gave it to her. She put it against her waist and let it fall from her hips, turning one way and the other. She was graceful and the skirt flowed around her like water, but I hated the Aleuts and took it from her.

"*Wintscha*," she said.

I had not heard words spoken for so long that they sounded strange to me, yet they were good to hear, even though it was an enemy who spoke them.

She said other words I did not understand, but now as she spoke she looked over my shoulder toward the cave. She pointed to the cave and then to me and made gestures as if she were making a fire. I knew what she wanted me to say, but I did not say it. She wished to know if I lived there in the cave so she could come back with the men and take me to their camp. I shook my head, and pointed to the far end of the island, away, away, for I did not trust her.

She kept looking toward the cave, but she said

nothing more about it. I held the spear, which I could have thrown. I did not, though I feared she would return with the hunters.

She came over to me and touched my arm. I did not like the feel of her hand. She said more words and smiled again and walked to the spring and drank. The next moment she had disappeared in the brush. Rontu did not try to follow her. She made no noise as she went.

I crawled back in the cave and began to pack the things I owned. I had all the day to do it, because the men were working and would not return to their camp before night.

By nightfall I was ready to go. I planned to take my canoe and go to the west part of the island. I could sleep there on the rocks until the Aleuts left, moving from place to place if I needed to.

I carried five baskets up the ravine and hid them near my house. It was getting dark and I had to go back to the cave for two that were left. Carefully I crawled through the brush and stopped just above the mouth of the cave and listened. Rontu was beside me and he listened also. No one could go through the brush in the dusk without making a sound, except someone who had lived in it for a long time.

I went past the spring and waited and then on to the cave. I felt that someone had been there while

I had been away. They could be hiding in the dark watching me. They were waiting until I went into the cave.

I was afraid so I did not go in, but quickly turned around. As I did so I saw something in front of the cave, on the flat rock I used for a step. It was a necklace of black stones of a kind I had never seen.

22

I DID NOT go into the cave nor did I take the necklace from the rock. That night I slept on the headland at the place where I had left my baskets. At dawn I went back to the ravine. There I hid myself on a brushy ledge. It was near the spring and from it I could see the mouth of the cave.

The sun rose and shone through the ravine. I could see the necklace lying on the rock. The stones looked blacker than they had in the darkness and there were many of them. I wanted to go down to the cave and count them, to see if they would make two loops around my neck, but I did not leave the ledge.

I stayed there all the morning. The sun was high when Rontu barked and I heard steps below me. The girl came out of the brush singing. She walked to the cave, but when she saw the necklace lying on the rock she grew quiet. She picked up the necklace and put it down again and peered into the mouth of the cave. Two of my baskets were still there. Then she went and drank from the spring and started off through the brush.

I jumped to my feet. "Tutok," I cried, running down the ravine. "Tutok."

She came out of the brush so quickly that she must have been waiting nearby to see if I would return.

I ran to the rock and put on the necklace and turned around for her to admire it. The beads made not two loops but three. They were long and oval instead of round, which is a very hard shape to make and takes much skill.

"*Wintscha*," she said.

"*Wintscha*," I said, after her, the word strange on my tongue. Then I said the word that meant pretty in our language.

"*Win-tai*," she said and laughed, because this was strange to her.

She touched the necklace, giving the word for it, and I gave mine. We pointed out other things — the spring, the cave, a gull flying, the sun and the sky, Rontu asleep — trading the names for them and laughing because they were so different. We sat there on the rock until the sun was in the west and played this game. Then Tutok rose and made a gesture of farewell.

"*Mah-nay*," she said and waited to hear my name.

"Won-a-pa-lei," I answered, which as I have said, means The Girl with the Long Black Hair. I did not tell her my secret name.

"*Mah-nay*, Won-a-pa-lei," she said.

"*Pah-say-no*, Tutok," I replied.

I watched her go through the brush. I stood for a long time listening to her footsteps, until I could hear them no more, and then I went to the headland and brought the baskets back to the cave.

Tutok came again the next day. We sat on the rock in the bright sun, trading words and laughing. The sun went fast in the sky. The time came soon when she had to leave, but she returned on the day that followed. It was on this day, when she was leaving, that I told her my secret name.

"Karana," I said, pointing to myself.

She repeated the word, but she did not understand what it meant.

"Won-a-pa-lei," she said, frowning.

I shook my head. Pointing again to myself, I said, "Karana."

Her black eyes opened wide. Slowly she began to smile.

"*Pah-say-no*, Karana," she said.

That night I began to make a gift for her, in return for the necklace she had given me. At first I thought I would give her a pair of my bone earrings, but remembering that her ears were not pierced and that I had a basket of abalone shells already flaked into thin disks, I set about making a circlet for her hair. I bored two holes in each of the disks, using thorns and fine sand. Between them I put ten olivella shells, which were no larger than the tip of my little finger, and threaded them all together with sinew.

I worked five nights on the circlet and on the fifth day when she came I gave it to her, putting it around her head and tying it in the back.

"*Wintscha*," she said and hugged me. She was so pleased that I forgot how sore my fingers were from boring the holes in the hard shells.

Many times she came to the cave, and then one morning she did not come. I waited for her all that day and at dusk I left the cave and went to the ledge where I could watch the ravine, fearing that the men had learned that I lived here and would find me. That night I slept on the ledge. The night was cold with the first wind of winter.

Tutok did not return the next day and I remembered that it was near the time when the Aleut hunters would leave. Perhaps they had already gone. That afternoon I went to the headland. I climbed the rock and crawled across it until I could look over the rim. My heart beat loud.

The Aleut ship was still there, but men were

working on the deck and canoes were going back and forth. The wind blew hard and few bales of otter skins lay on the shore so probably the ship would leave at dawn.

It was dark when I got back to the ravine. Since the wind was very cold and I was no longer afraid that the Aleuts would find me, I made a fire in the cave and cooked a supper of shellfish and roots. I cooked enough for Rontu and me and for Tutok. I knew Tutok would not come, yet I put her food beside the fire and waited.

Once Rontu barked and I thought I heard the sound of footsteps and went to the opening and listened. I waited a long while and did not eat. Clouds moved from the north, covering the cold sky. The wind grew louder and made wild noises in the ravine. At last I closed the mouth of the cave with stones.

At dawn I went to the headland. The wind had died. Fog lay over the sea, washing against the island in gray waves. I waited a long time for a glimpse of Coral Cove, but finally the sun burned away the fog. The little harbor was deserted. The Aleut ship with its red-beaked prow and red sails had gone.

At first, knowing that I could now leave the cave and move back into my house on the headland, I was happy. But as I stood there on the high rock looking down at the deserted harbor and the empty sea, I began to think of Tutok. I thought of all the times we had sat in the sun together. I could hear her voice and see her black eyes squinting closed when she laughed.

Below me, Rontu was running along the cliff, barking at the screaming gulls. Pelicans were chattering as they fished the blue water. Far off I could hear the bellow of a sea elephant. But suddenly, as I thought of Tutok, the island seemed very quiet.

23

THE HUNTERS left many wounded otter behind them. Some floated in and died on the shore and others I killed with my spear since they were suffering and could not live. But I found a young otter that was not badly hurt.

It lay in a bed of bull kelp and I would have paddled by if Rontu had not barked. A strand of kelp was wound around its body and I thought it was sleeping, for often before they go to sleep they anchor themselves in this way to keep from drifting off. Then I saw there was a deep gash across its back.

The otter did not try to swim away as I drew near and reached over the side of the canoe. They have large eyes, especially when they are young, but this one's were so large from fear and pain that I could see my reflection in them. I cut the kelp that held it and took it to a tide pool behind the reef, which was sheltered from the waves.

The day was calm after the storm and I caught two fish along the reef. I was careful to keep them alive, because otter will not eat anything that is dead, and left them in the pool. This was early in the morning.

That afternoon I went back to the pool. The fish had disappeared and the young otter was asleep, floating on its back. I did not try to treat its wound with herbs because salt water heals and the herbs would have washed off anyway.

I brought two fish every day and left them in the pool. The otter would not eat while I was watching. Then I brought four fish and these also disappeared and finally six, which seemed to be the right number. I brought them whether the day was calm or stormy.

The otter grew and its wound began to heal, but still it stayed in the pool, and now when I came it would be waiting for me and would take the fish from my hand. The pool was not big and it could easily have gotten out and away into the sea, yet it stayed there and slept or waited for me to come with food.

The young otter now was the length of my arm and very glossy. It had a long nose that came to a point and many whiskers on each side and the largest eyes I have ever seen. They would watch me all the time I was at the pool, following me whatever I did, and when I said something, they would move around in a very funny way. In a way, too, that made pain come to my throat because they were gay and sad also.

For a long time I called it Otter as I had called Rontu, Dog. Then I decided to give the otter a name. The name was Mon-a-nee, which means Little Boy with Large Eyes.

It was a hard task catching fish every day, especially if the wind was blowing and the waves were high. Once when I could catch only two and dropped them into the pool, Mon-a-nee ate them quickly and waited for more. When he found that was all I had he swam around in circles, looking at me reproachfully.

The waves were so high the next day that I could not fish on the reef even at low tide, and since I had nothing to give him I did not go to the pool.

It was three days before I could catch fish and when I went there again the pool was deserted. I knew that he would leave someday, but I felt bad that he had gone back to the sea and that I would never catch fish for him again. Nor would I know him if I saw him again in the kelp, for now that he had grown and his wound had healed, he looked like all the others.

Soon after the Aleuts had left I moved back to the headland.

Nothing had been harmed except the fence, which I mended, and in a few days the house was the same as before. The only thing that worried me was that all the abalones I had gathered in the summer were gone. I would need to live from day to day on what I could catch, trying to get enough on the days when I could fish to last through the times when I could not. Through the first part of the winter, before Mon-a-nee swam away, this was sometimes hard to do. Afterwards it was not so hard and Rontu and I always had enough to eat.

While the Aleuts were on the island, I had no chance to catch little smelts and dry them, so the nights that winter were dark and I went to bed early and worked only during the day. But still I made another string for my fishing spear, many hooks of abalone shell, and last of all earrings to match the necklace Tutok had given me.

These took a long time, for I searched the beach many mornings when the tide was out before I found two pebbles of the same color as the stones in the necklace and soft enough to cut. The holes in the earrings took even more time, for the stones were hard to hold, but when I was done and had rubbed them bright in fine sand and water, and fastened them with bone hooks to fit my ears, they were very pretty.

On sunny days I would wear them with my cormorant dress and the necklace, and walk along the cliff with Rontu.

I often thought of Tutok, but on these days especially I would look off into the north and wish that she were here to see me. I could hear her talking in her strange language and I would make up things to say to her and things for her to say to me.

24

SPRING AGAIN was a time of flowers and water ran in the ravines and flowed down to the sea. Many birds came back to the island.

Tainor and Lurai built a nest in the tree where they were born. They built it of dry seaweed and leaves and also with hairs off Rontu's back. Whenever he was in the yard while it was being made, they would swoop down if he were not looking and snatch a beakful of fur and fly away. This he did not like and he finally hid from them until the nest was finished.

I had been right in giving a girl's name to Lurai, for she laid speckled eggs and, with some help from her mate, hatched two ugly fledglings which soon became beautiful. I made up names for them and clipped their wings and before long they were as tame as their parents.

I also found a young gull that had fallen from its

nest to the beach below. Gulls make their nests high on the cliffs, in hollow places on the rocks. These places are usually small and often I had watched a young one teetering on the edge of the nest and wondered why it did not fall. They seldom did.

This one, which was white with a yellow beak, was not badly hurt, but he had a broken leg. I took him back to the house and bound the bones together with two small sticks and sinew. For a while he did not try to walk. Then, because he was not old enough to fly, he began to hobble around the yard.

With the young birds and the old ones, the white gull and Rontu, who was always trotting at my heels, the yard seemed a happy place. If only I had not remembered Tutok. If only I had not wondered about my sister Ulape, where she was, and if the marks she had drawn upon her cheeks had proved magical. If they had, she was now married to Kimko and was the mother of many children. She would have smiled to see all of mine, which were so different from the ones I always wished to have.

Early that spring I started to gather abalones and I gathered many, taking them to the headland to dry. I wanted to have a good supply ready if the Aleuts came again.

One day when I was on the reef filling my canoe,

I saw a herd of otter in the kelp nearby. They were chasing each other, putting their heads through the kelp and then going under and coming up again in a different place. It was like a game we used to play in the brush when there were children on the island. I looked for Mon-a-nee, but each of them was like the other.

I filled my canoe with abalones and paddled toward shore, one of the otter following me. As I stopped he dived and came up in front of me. He was far away, yet even then I knew who it was. I never thought that I would be able to tell him from the others, but I was so sure it was Mon-a-nee that I held up one of the fish I had caught.

Otter swim very fast and before I could take a breath, he had snatched it from my hand.

For two moons I did not see him and then one morning while I was fishing he came suddenly out of the kelp. Behind him were two baby otter. They were about the size of puppies and they moved along so slowly that from time to time Mon-a-nee had to urge them on. Sea otter cannot swim when they are first born, and have to hold on to their mother. Little by little she teaches her babies by brushing them away with her flippers, then swimming around them in circles until they learn to follow.

Mon-a-nee came close to the reef and I threw a

fish into the water. He did not snatch it as he usually did, but waited to see what the young otter would do. When they seemed more interested in me than in food, and the fish started to swim away, he seized it with his sharp teeth and tossed it in front of them.

I threw another fish into the water for Mon-a-nee, but he did the same things as before. Still the babies would not take the food, and at last, tired of playing with it, swam over and began to nuzzle him.

Only then did I know that Mon-a-nee was their mother. Otter mate for life and if the mother dies the father will often raise the babies as best he can. This is what I thought had happened to Mon-a-nee.

I looked down at the little family swimming beside the reef. "Mon-a-nee," I said, "I am going to give you a new name. It is Won-a-nee, which fits you because it means Girl with the Large Eyes."

The young otter grew fast and soon were taking fish from my hand, but Won-a-nee liked abalones better. She would let the abalone I tossed to her sink to the bottom and then dive and come up holding it against her body, with a rock held in her mouth. Then she would float on her back and put the abalone on her breast and strike it again and again with the rock until the shell was broken.

She taught her young to do this and sometimes

I sat on the reef all the morning and watched the three of them pounding the hard shells against their breasts. If all otters did not eat abalones this way I would have thought it was a game played by Won-a-nee just to please me. But they all did and I always wondered about it, and I wonder to this time.

After that summer, after being friends with Won-a-nee and her young, I never killed another otter. I had an otter cape for my shoulders, which I used until it wore out, but never again did I make a new one. Nor did I ever kill another cormorant for its beautiful feathers, though they have long, thin necks and make ugly sounds when they talk to each other. Nor did I kill seals for their sinews, using instead kelp to bind the things that needed it. Nor did I kill another wild dog, nor did I try to spear another sea elephant.

Ulape would have laughed at me, and others would have laughed, too — my father most of all. Yet this is the way I felt about the animals who had become my friends and those who were not, but in time could be. If Ulape and my father had come back and laughed, and all the others had come back and laughed, still I would have felt the same way, for animals and birds are like people, too, though they do not talk the same or do the same things. Without them the earth would be an unhappy place.

25

THE ALEUTS never again came to the Island of the Blue Dolphins, but every summer I watched for them, and early every spring I gathered shellfish, which I dried and stored in the cave where I kept my canoe.

Two winters after they left I made more weapons — a spear, a bow, and a quiver of arrows. These I also stored in the place beneath the headland, so if the hunters returned I would be ready to go to another part of the island, to move from cave to cave, living in my canoe if necessary.

For many summers after the Aleuts had gone the herd of otter left Coral Cove. The old otter which had survived the Aleut spears and by now were aware that summer was a time of danger would lead the herd away. They went far off to the kelp beds of Tall Rock where they stayed until the first storms of winter

Often Rontu and I would go out to the rock and live there for several days catching fish for Won-a-nee and the others I had come to know.

One summer the otter did not leave, the summer that Rontu died, and I knew then that none of the otter who remembered the hunters were left. Nor did I think of them often nor of the white men who had said they would come back, but did not come.

Until that summer, I had kept count of all the moons since the time my brother and I were alone upon the island. For each one that came and went I cut a mark in a pole beside the door of my house. There were many marks, from the roof to the floor. But after that summer I did not cut them any more. The passing of the moons now had come to mean little, and I only made marks to count the four seasons of the year. The last year I did not count those.

It was late in the summer that Rontu died. The days since spring, whenever I went to the reef to fish, he would not go with me unless I urged him to. He liked to lie in the sun in front of the house and I let him, but I did not go so often as in the past.

I remember the night that Rontu stood at the fence and barked for me to let him out. Usually he did this when the moon was big, and he came back in the morning, but that night there was no moon and he did not return.

I waited all that day for him until almost dusk and then I went out to look for him. I saw his tracks and followed them over the dunes and a hill to the lair where he had once lived. There I found him, lying in the back of the cave, alone. At first I thought that he had been hurt, yet there were no wounds on him. He touched my hand with his tongue, but only once and then he was quiet and scarcely breathed.

Since night had fallen and it was too dark for me to carry Rontu back, I stayed there. I sat beside him through the night and talked to him. At dawn I took him in my arms and left the cave. He was very light, as if something about him had already gone.

The sun was up as I went along the cliff. Gulls were crying in the sky. He raised his ears at the sound, and I put him down, thinking that he wished to bark at them as he always did. He raised his head and followed them with his eyes, but did not make a sound.

"Rontu," I said, "you have always liked to bark at the seagulls. Whole mornings and afternoons you have barked at them. Bark at them now for me."

But he did not look at them again. Slowly he walked to where I was standing and fell at my feet. I put my hand on his chest. I could feel his heart beating, but it beat only twice, very slowly, loud and hollow like the waves on the beach, and then no more.

"Rontu," I cried, "oh, Rontu!"

I buried him on the headland. I dug a hole in the crevice of the rock, digging for two days from dawn until the going down of the sun, and put him there with some sand flowers and a stick he liked to chase when I threw it, and covered him with pebbles of many colors that I gathered on the shore.

26

THAT WINTER I did not go to the reef at all. I ate the things I had stored and left the house only to get water at the spring. It was a winter of strong winds and rain and wild seas that crashed against the cliffs, so I would not have gone out much even if Rontu had been there. During that time I made four snares from notched branches.

In the summer once, when I was on my way to the place where the sea elephants lived, I had seen a young dog that looked like Rontu. He was running with one of the packs of wild dogs, and though I caught only a glimpse of him, I was sure he was Rontu's son.

He was larger than the other dogs and had heavier fur and yellow eyes and he ran with a graceful stride like Rontu's. In the spring I planned to catch him with the snares I was making.

The wild dogs came to the headland often during

the winter, now that Rontu was gone, and when the worst of the storms were over I set the snares outside the fence and baited them with fish. I caught several of the dogs the first time, but not the one with the yellow eyes, and since I was afraid to handle them, I was forced to let them free.

I made more snares and set these again, but while the wild dogs came close they would not touch the fish. I did catch a little red fox, which bit me when I took her out of the snare, yet she soon got over her wildness and would follow me around in the yard, begging for abalone. She was very much of a thief. When I was away from the house, she always found some way to get into the food, no matter how well I hid it, so I had to let her go back to the ravine. Often, though, she would come at night and scratch at the fence for food.

I could not catch the young dog with a snare, and I was about to give up trying to when I thought of the toluache weed which we sometimes used to catch fish in the tide pools. It was not really a poison, but if you put it in the water the fish would turn over on their backs and float.

I remembered this weed and dug some where it grew on the far side of the island. I broke it up into small pieces which I dropped in the spring where the wild dogs drank. I waited all day and at dusk the pack came down to the spring. They drank their fill of the water, but nothing happened to them, or not much. They frisked around for a while, as I watched them from the brush, and trotted away.

I then remembered xuchal, which some of the men of our tribe used and is made from ground-up sea shells and wild tobacco. I made a big bowl of this, mixing it with water, and put it in the spring. I hid in the brush and waited. The dogs came at dusk. They sniffed the water and backed off and looked at each other, but at last began to drink. Soon afterwards they began to walk around in circles. Suddenly they all lay down and went to sleep.

There were nine of them lying there by the spring. In the dim light it was hard to tell the one I wanted to take home, but finally I found him. He was snoring as if he had just eaten a big meal. I picked him up and hurried along the cliff, being frightened all the way that he would wake up before I reached the headland.

I pulled him through the opening under the fence and tied him to it with a thong and left food beside him to eat and some fresh water. Before long he was on his feet, gnawing through the thong. He howled and ran about the yard while I cooked my supper. All night he howled, but at dawn when I went out of the house, he was asleep.

While he lay there by the fence sleeping, I

thought of different names for him, trying first one and then another, saying them over to myself. At last, because he looked so much like his father, I called him Rontu-Aru, which means Son of Rontu.

In a short time he made friends with me. He was not so large as Rontu, but he had his father's thick coat and the same yellow eyes. Often when I watched him chasing gulls on the sandspit or on the reef barking at the otter, I forgot that he was not Rontu.

We had many happy times that summer, fishing and going to Tall Rock in our canoe, but more and more now I thought of Tutok and my sister Ulape. Sometimes I would hear their voices in the wind and often, when I was on the sea, in the waves that lapped softly against the canoe.

27

After the fierce storms of winter came many days when the wind did not blow. The air was so heavy that it was hard to breathe and the sun so hot that the sea was like a sun itself, too bright to look at.

The last day of this weather I took the canoe from the cave and paddled around the reef to the sandspit. I did not take Rontu-Aru with me, for while he liked the cold he did not like heat. It was good that he did not come with me. The day was the hottest of all and the sea shimmered with red light. Over my eyes I wore shields made of wood with small slits in them to see through. No gulls were flying, the otter lay quiet in the kelp, and the little crabs were deep in their holes.

I pulled the canoe up on the beach, which was wet but steaming from the sun. Early every spring I took the canoe to the sandspit and spread fresh pitch in the cracks that needed it. I worked all this morning, stopping from time to time to cool off in the sea. As the sun climbed high I turned the canoe over and crawled under it and went to sleep in the shade.

I had not slept long when I was suddenly awakened by what I thought was thunder, but upon looking out from my shelter I saw that there were no clouds in the sky. Yet the rumbling sound kept on. It came from a distance, from the south and, as I listened, grew louder.

I jumped to my feet. The first thing that caught my gaze was the gleaming stretch of beach on the southern slope of the sandspit. Never in my life on the island had I seen the tide so low. Rocks and small reefs that I did not know were under the sea stood bare in the blinding light. It was like another place. I had gone to sleep and wakened on another island.

The air was suddenly tight around me. There was a faint sound as if some giant animal were sucking the air in and in through its teeth. The rumbling came closer out of an empty sky, filling my ears. Then beyond the gleam of the beach and the bare rocks and reefs, more than a league beyond them, I saw a great white crest moving down upon the island.

It seemed to move slowly between the sea and the sky, but it was the sea itself. I tore off the shields I wore over my eyes. In terror I ran along the sand-spit. I ran and stumbled and got up and ran again. The sand shuddered under my feet as the first wave struck. Spray fell around me like rain. It was filled with pieces of kelp and small fish.

By following the curve of the sandspit I could reach the cove and the trail that led to the mesa, but there was no time for this. Water was already rush-ing around my knees, pulling from every direction. The cliff rose in front of me and though the rocks were slippery with sea moss I found a hold for a hand and then a foot. Thus, a step at a time, I dragged myself upward.

The crest of the wave passed under me and roared on toward Coral Cove.

For a time there was no sound. Then the sea began to seek its old place, running backward in long, foaming currents. Before it could do so an-other great wave moved out of the south. Perhaps it would be even bigger than the first one. I looked up. The cliff rose straight above me. I could climb no farther.

I stood facing the rock, with my feet on a narrow ledge and one hand thrust deep into a crack. Over my shoulder I could see the wave coming. It did not come fast, for the other wave was still running out. For a while I thought that it would not come at all because the two suddenly met beyond the sandspit.

The first wave was trying to reach the sea and the second one was struggling toward the shore.

Like two giants they crashed against each other. They rose high in the air, bending first one way and then the other. There was a roar as if great spears were breaking in battle and in the red light of the sun the spray that flew around them looked like blood.

Slowly the second wave forced the first one backward, rolled slowly over it, and then as a victor drags the vanquished, moved in toward the island.

The wave struck the cliff. It sent long tongues streaming around me so that I could neither see nor hear. The tongues of water licked into all the crevices, dragged at my hand and at my bare feet gripping the ledge. They rose high above me along the face of the rock, up and up, and then spent themselves against the sky and fell back, hissing past me to join the water rushing on toward the cove.

Suddenly all around me was quiet. In the quiet I could hear my heart pounding and knew that my hand still had its hold on the rock and that I was alive.

Night came and though I was afraid to leave the cliff I knew that I could never stay there until morning, that I would go to sleep and fall. Neither could I find my way home, so I climbed down from the ledge and crouched at the foot of the cliff.

Dawn was windless and hot. The sandspit was strewn with hills of kelp. Dead fish and lobsters and pink crabs lay everywhere, and two small whales were stranded against the rock walls of the cove. Far up the trail that led to the mesa I found things from the sea.

Rontu-Aru was waiting at the fence. When I crawled under it he jumped upon me and followed me around, never letting me out of his sight.

I was glad to be home on the high headland where the waves had not come. I had been gone only from one sun to the next, yet it was like many suns, like the time I had gone away in the canoe. Most of the day I slept, but I had many dreams and when I awoke everything around me was strange. The sea made no sounds on the shore. The gulls were quiet. The earth seemed to be holding its breath, as though it were waiting for something terrible to happen.

At dusk I was coming back from the spring with a basket of water on my shoulder, walking along the cliff with Rontu-Aru. Everywhere, the ocean was smooth and yellow and it lay against the island as if it were very tired. The gulls were still quiet, perched on their rocky nests.

Slowly the earth began to move. It moved away from my feet and for a moment I seemed to be standing in the air. Water tipped out of the basket and trickled over my face. Then the basket fell to the ground. Not knowing what I did, thinking foolishly that another wave was upon me, I began to run. But it *was* a wave, a wave of earth, and it rippled under me along the cliff.

As I ran another wave overtook me. Looking back I saw many of them coming out of the south like waves in the sea. The next thing I remember I was lying on the ground and Rontu-Aru was beside me and we were both trying to get to our feet. Then we were running again toward the headland, toward a house that kept moving off into the distance.

The opening under the fence had caved in and I had to pull the rocks away before we could crawl through. Night came, but the earth still rose and fell like a great animal breathing. I could hear rocks tumbling from the cliff, falling down into the sea.

All night as we lay there in the house the earth trembled and rocks fell, yet not the big one on the headland, which would have fallen if those who make the world shake had really been angry with us.

In the morning the earth was quiet once more and a fresh wind that smelled of kelp blew out of the northern sea.

28

The earthquake did little damage. Even the spring, which failed to flow for several days, started up again and flowed more than ever. But the great waves had cost me all the food and weapons which were stored in the cave, as well as the canoe I had been working on and those hidden under the south cliffs.

The canoes were the biggest loss. To find enough wood to make another would have taken me all the spring and summer. I therefore set out on the first fair morning to search for whatever wreckage the waves had washed ashore.

Among the rocks near the south cliffs I found a part of one canoe, buried in sand and twisted kelp. I worked all morning to dig it free and then, having scraped it clean, could not decide what to do. I could cut the sinews and carry the planks up the cliff two at a time on my back and across the dunes to Coral Cove, which meant many days. Or I could build the canoe here on the rocks and take the chance that another storm would wash it away before I was finished.

I finally did neither of these things. Choosing a day when the sea was calm, I floated what was left of the canoe and, pushing it in front of me, made my way past the sandspit and into the cove. There I took the wreckage apart and moved the planks up the trail, beyond the place where the great waves had reached.

I found the remains of my other canoe. It had been washed far back in the cave and I could not get it out, so I went back to the south cliffs and hunted among the piles of kelp until I had enough pieces of wood, counting what I already had, to begin the building of another.

It was late in the spring now. The weather was still unsettled, with light rain falling most of the days, but I started the new canoe anyway, for I needed it to gather shellfish. No longer did I think of the Aleuts, as I have said, yet without a canoe to go where I wanted, I felt uneasy.

The planks were all about the same size, the length of my arm, but they came from different canoes and were therefore hard to fit together. The holes were ready, however, which saved me much labor and time. Another help was that the great waves had washed ashore long strings of black pitch, which was often difficult to find on the island and which I needed.

When I had sorted out the planks and shaped them, the work went fast, so that by late spring I was ready to finish the seams. It was on a windy morning that I made a fire to soften the pitch. The wind was cold and it took a long time to get the fire going. To hasten it I went down to the beach for dry seaweed.

I had started back with my arms filled when I turned to look at the sky, thinking from the feel of the wind that a storm might be close. Off to the north the skies were clear, but in the east from whence storms sometimes came at this season, stood banks of gray clouds, one on top of the other.

At this moment, in the deep shadows cast by the clouds, I saw something else. Forgetting that I was carrying a load of seaweed, I threw up my arms. The seaweed fell to the ground.

A sail, a ship, was there on the sea, halfway between the horizon and the shore!

By the time I had reached the headland it was much closer, moving quickly on the strong wind. I could see that it did not have the red, beaked prow of the Aleuts. Nor did it look like the white men's ship, which I clearly remembered.

Why had it come to the Island of the Blue Dolphins?

I crouched on the headland and wondered, my heart beating fast, if the men who sailed it had come to catch otter. If they were hunters, I must hide before they saw me. They would soon find my fire and the canoe I was making, yet I could go to the cave and probably be safe from them. But if they had been sent by my people to take me away, then I should not hide.

The ship moved slowly between the black rocks and into Coral Cove. I could see the men now and they were not Aleuts.

They lowered a canoe and two of the men paddled toward the beach. The wind had begun to blow hard and the men had trouble landing. Finally one of them stayed behind in the canoe, and the other, the man without a beard, jumped into the water and came along the beach and up the trail.

I could not see him, but after a while I heard a shout, then another, and I knew that he had found my fire and the canoe. The man he had left in the cove did not answer, nor did the men on the ship, so I was sure that he was calling to me.

I crawled down from the rock and went to the house. Since my shoulders were bare, I put on my otter cape. I took my cormorant skirt and the abalone box in which I kept my necklace and earrings.

With Rontu-Aru I then went along the trail that led to Coral Cove.

I came to the mound where my ancestors had sometimes camped in the summer. I thought of them and of the happy times spent in my house on the headland, of my canoe lying unfinished beside the trail. I thought of many things, but stronger was the wish to be where people lived, to hear their voices and their laughter.

I left the mound and the green grass growing on it among the white shells. I could no longer hear the man calling, so I began to run. When I came to the place where the two trails met, where I had built my fire, I found the footsteps the man had left.

I followed them down to the cove. The canoe had gone back to the ship. The wind was screaming now and mist blew in across the harbor and waves began to pile up on the shore. I raised my hand and shouted. I shouted over and over, but the wind carried my voice away. I ran down the beach and waded into the water. The men did not see me.

Rain started to fall and the wind drove it against my face. I waded farther out through the waves, raising my arms to the ship. Slowly it moved away in the mist. It went toward the south. I stood there until it was out of sight.

29

A**FTER TWO MORE** springs had gone, on a morning of
white clouds and calm seas, the ship came back. At
dawn I saw it from the headland far out on the
horizon. When the sun was overhead it lay anchored in Coral Cove.

Until the sun went down I watched from the
headland while the men made a camp on the shore
and built a fire. Then I went to my house. All
night I did not sleep, thinking of the man who once
had called to me.

I had thought of his voice calling for a long time,
since the night of the storm when the ship had
sailed away. Every day during those two springs and
two summers I had gone to the headland and
watched, always at dawn and again at dusk.

In the morning I smelled smoke from their fire.
I went down to the ravine and bathed in the spring
and put on my otter cape and my cormorant skirt

I put on the necklace of black stones and the black earrings. With blue clay I made the mark of our tribe across my nose.

Then I did something that made me smile at myself. I did what my older sister Ulape had done when she left the Island of the Blue Dolphins. Below the mark of our tribe I carefully made the sign which meant that I was still unmarried. I was no longer a girl, yet I made it anyway, using the blue clay and some white clay for the dots.

I went back to the house then and built a fire and cooked food for Rontu-Aru and me. I was not hungry and he ate my food and his too.

"We are going away," I said to him, "away from our island."

But he only put his head to one side, as his father often had done, and when I said no more, he trotted out to a sunny place and lay down and fell asleep.

Now that the white men had come back, I could not think of what I would do when I went across the sea, or make a picture in my mind of the white men and what they did there, or see my people who had been gone so long. Nor, thinking of the past, of the many summers and winters and springs that had gone, could I see each of them. They were all one, a tight feeling in my breast and nothing more.

The morning was full of sun. The wind smelled of the sea and the things that lived in it. I saw the men long before they saw the house on the headland, far off on the dunes to the south. There were three of them, two tall men and one who was short and wore a long gray robe. They left the dunes and came along the cliff, and then seeing the smoke from the fire which I kept burning, they followed it, and at last reached my house.

I crawled under the fence and stood facing them. The man in the gray robe had a string of beads around his neck and at the end of it was an ornament of polished wood. He raised his hand and made a motion toward me which was the shape of the ornament he wore. Then one of the two men who stood behind him spoke to me. His words made the strangest sounds I have ever heard. At first I wanted to laugh, but I bit my tongue.

I shook my head and smiled at him. He spoke again, slowly this time, and though his words sounded the same as before and meant nothing to me, they now seemed sweet. They were the sound of a human voice. There is no sound like this in all the world.

The man lifted his hand and pointed toward the cove and made a picture in the air of what could have been a ship.

To this I nodded and myself pointed to the three baskets I had placed by the fire, making a gesture of taking them with me to the ship. Also the cage in which I had put two young birds.

There were many gestures before we left, though the two men spoke among themselves. They liked my necklace, the cape, and the cormorant skirt that shone in the sun. But when we got to the beach, where their camp was, the first thing the man who spoke the most did was to tell the other men to make me a dress.

I knew this was what he said because one of them stood in front of me and held up a string from my neck to my feet and across my shoulders.

The dress was blue. It was made of two trousers, just like those the white men were wearing. The trousers were cut up into pieces and then one of the men sat down on a rock and put them together again with white string. He had a long nose, which looked like the needle he used. He sat all afternoon on the rock and the needle went back and forth, in and out, flashing in the sun.

From time to time he would hold up the dress and nod his head as if he were pleased. I nodded as if I were pleased, too, but I was not. I wanted to wear my cormorant skirt and my otter cape, which were much more beautiful than the thing he was making.

The dress reached from my throat to my feet and

I did not like it, either the color of it or the way it scratched. It was also hot. But I smiled and put my cormorant skirt away in one of the baskets to wear when I got across the sea, sometime when the men were not around.

The ship stayed in Coral Cove nine days. It had come for otter, but the otter had gone. Some must have been left, after all, who remembered the Aleuts, for on that morning there were none to be seen.

I knew where they had gone. They had gone to Tall Rock, but when the men showed me the weapons they had brought to kill the otter, I shook my head and acted as though I did not understand. They pointed to my otter cape, but I still shook my head.

I asked them then about the ship that had taken my people away many years before, making the signs of the ship and pointing to the east, but they did not understand. Not until I came to Mission Santa Barbara and met Father Gonzales did I learn from him that this ship had sunk in a great storm soon after it reached his country and that on the whole ocean thereabouts there was no other. For this reason, the white men had not come back for me.

On the tenth day we sailed. It was a morning of

blue skies and no wind. We went straight toward the sun.

For a long time I stood and looked back at the Island of the Blue Dolphins. The last thing I saw of it was the high headland. I thought of Rontu lying there beneath the stones of many colors, and of Won-a-nee, wherever she was, and the little red fox that would scratch in vain at my fence, and my canoe hidden in the cave, and of all the happy days.

Dolphins rose out of the sea and swam before the ship. They swam for many leagues in the morning through the bright water, weaving their foamy patterns. The little birds were chirping in their cage and Rontu-Aru sat beside me.

Author's Note

T<small>HE ISLAND</small> called in this book the Island of the
Blue Dolphins was first settled by Indians in about
2000 B.C., but it was not discovered by white men
until 1602.

In that year the Spanish explorer Sebastián Viz-
caíno set out from Mexico in search of a port where
treasure galleons from the Philippines could find
shelter in case of distress. Sailing north along the
California coast, he sighted the island, sent a small
boat ashore and named it La Isla de San Nicolas, in
honor of the patron saint of sailors, travelers, and
merchants.

As the centuries passed, California changed from
Spanish to Mexican hands, the Americans arrived,
but only occasional hunters visited the island. Its
Indian inhabitants remained in isolation.

The girl Robinson Crusoe whose story I have
attempted to re-create actually lived alone upon

this island from 1835 to 1853, and is known to history as The Lost Woman of San Nicolas.

The facts about her are few. From the reports of Captain Hubbard, whose schooner carried away the Indians of Ghalas-at, we know that the girl did jump into the sea, despite efforts to restrain her. From records left by Captain Nidever we know that he found her eighteen years later, alone with a dog in a crude house on the headland, dressed in a skirt of cormorant feathers. Father Gonzales of Santa Barbara Mission, who befriended her after her rescue, learned that her brother had been killed by wild dogs. He learned little else, for she spoke to him only in signs; neither he nor the many Indians at the mission could understand her strange language. The Indians of Ghalas-at had long since disappeared.

The Lost Woman of San Nicolas is buried on a hill near the Santa Barbara Mission. Her skirt of green cormorant feathers was sent to Rome.

Outermost of the eight Channel Islands, San Nicolas is about seventy-five miles southwest of Los Angeles. For years historians thought that it had been settled some six centuries ago, but recent carbon-14 tests of excavations on the island show that Indians came here from the north long before the Christian era. Their images of the creatures of the land, sea, and air, similar to those found on the shores of Alaska and carved with extraordinary skill, may be seen at the Southwest Museum in Los Angeles.

The future of San Nicolas is not clear. It is now a secret base of the United States Navy, but scientists predict that because of the pounding waves and furious winds it will one day be swept back into the sea.

In the writing of the *Island of the Blue Dolphins*, I am deeply indebted to Maude and Delos Lovelace, to Bernice Eastman Johnson of the Southwest Museum, and to Fletcher Carr, formerly curator of the San Diego Museum of Man.

Turn the page for a special preview
of the

1996 NEWBERY HONOR BOOK

The Watsons Go to Birmingham—1963

CHRISTOPHER PAUL CURTIS

(ISBN 0-385-32175-9)

Enter the hilarious world of ten-year-old Kenny and his family, the Weird Watsons of Flint, Michigan. There's Momma, Dad, little sister Joetta, Kenny, and Byron, who's thirteen and an "official juvenile delinquent." When Momma and Dad decide it's time for a visit to Grandma, Dad comes home with the amazing Ultra-Glide, and the Watsons set out on a trip like no other. They're heading south. They're going to Birmingham, Alabama, toward one of the darkest moments in American history.

**Don't miss *The Watsons Go to Birmingham–1963*
by Christopher Paul Curtis.
On sale now from Delacorte Press!**

1. And You Wonder Why We Get Called the Weird Watsons

I t was one of those super-duper-cold Saturdays. One of those days that when you breathed out your breath kind of hung frozen in the air like a hunk of smoke and you could walk along and look exactly like a train blowing out big, fat, white puffs of smoke.

It was so cold that if you were stupid enough to go outside your eyes would automatically blink a thousand times all by themselves, probably so the juice inside of them wouldn't freeze up. It was so cold that if you spit, the slob would be an ice cube before it hit the ground. It was about a zillion degrees below zero.

It was even cold inside our house. We put sweaters and hats and scarves and three pairs of socks on and still were cold. The thermostat was turned all the way up and the furnace was banging and sounding like it was about to blow up but it still felt like Jack Frost had moved in with us.

All of my family sat real close together on the couch under a blanket. Dad said this would generate a little heat but he didn't have to tell us this, it seemed like the cold automatically made us want to get together and huddle up. My little sister, Joetta, sat in the middle and all you could see were her eyes because she had a scarf wrapped around her head. I was next to her, and on the outside was my mother.

Momma was the only one who wasn't born in Flint so the cold was coldest to her. All you could see were her eyes too, and they were shooting bad looks at Dad. She always blamed him for bringing her all the way from Alabama to Michigan, a state she called a giant icebox. Dad was bundled up on the other side of Joey, trying to look at anything but Momma. Next to Dad, sitting with a little space between them, was my older brother, Byron.

Byron had just turned thirteen so he was officially a teenage juvenile delinquent and didn't think it was "cool" to touch anybody or let anyone touch him, even if it meant he froze to death. Byron had tucked the blanket between him and Dad down into the cushion of the couch to make sure he couldn't be touched.

Dad turned on the TV to try to make us forget how cold we were but all that did was get him in trouble. There was a special news report on Channel 12 telling about how bad the weather was and Dad groaned when the guy said, "If you think it's cold now, wait until tonight, the temperature is expected to drop into record-low territory, possibly reaching the negative twenties! In fact, we won't be seeing anything above zero for the next four to five days!" He was smiling when he said this but none of the Watson family thought it was funny. We all looked over at Dad. He just shook his head and pulled the blanket over his eyes.

Then the guy on TV said, "Here's a little something we can use to brighten our spirits and give us some hope for the future: The temperature in Atlanta, Georgia, is forecast to reach . . ." Dad coughed real loud and jumped off the couch to turn the TV off but we all heard the weatherman say, ". . . the mid-seventies!" The guy might as well have tied Dad to a tree and said, "Ready, aim, fire!"

"Atlanta!" Momma said. "That's a hundred and fifty miles from home!"

"Wilona . . . ," Dad said.

"I knew it," Momma said. "I knew I should have listened to Moses Henderson!"

"Who?" I asked.

Dad said, "Oh Lord, not that sorry story. You've got to let me tell about what happened with him."

Momma said, "There's not a whole lot to tell, just a story about a young girl who made a bad choice. But if you do tell it, make sure you get all the facts right."

We all huddled as close as we could get because we knew Dad was going to try to make us forget about being cold by cutting up. Me and Joey started smiling right away, and Byron tried to look cool and bored.

"Kids," Dad said, "I almost wasn't your father. You guys came real close to having a clown for a daddy named Hambone Henderson. . . ."

"Daniel Watson, you stop right there. You're the one

who started that 'Hambone' nonsense. Before you started that everyone called him his Christian name, Moses. And he was a respectable boy too, he wasn't a clown at all."

"But the name stuck, didn't it? Hambone Henderson. Me and your granddaddy called him that because the boy had a head shaped just like a hambone, had more knots and bumps on his head than a dinosaur. So as you guys sit here giving me these dirty looks because it's a little chilly outside ask yourselves if you'd rather be a little cool or go through life being known as the Hambonettes."

Me and Joey cracked up, Byron kind of chuckled and Momma put her hand over her mouth. She did this whenever she was going to give a smile because she had a great big gap between her front teeth. If Momma thought something was funny, first you'd see her trying to keep her lips together to hide the gap, then, if the smile got to be too strong, you'd see the gap for a hot second before Momma's hand would come up to cover it, then she'd crack up too.

Laughing only encouraged Dad to cut up more, so when he saw the whole family thinking he was funny he really started putting on a show.

He stood in front of the TV. "Yup, Hambone Henderson proposed to your mother around the same time I did. Fought dirty too, told your momma a pack of lies about me and when she didn't believe them he told her a pack of lies about Flint."

Dad started talking Southern-style, imitating this

Hambone guy. "Wilona, I heard tell about the weather up that far north in Flint, Mitch-again, heard it's colder than inside a icebox. Seen a movie about it, think it was made in Flint. Movie called *Nanook of the North*. Yup, do believe for sure it was made in Flint. Uh-huh, Flint, Mitch-again.

"Folks there live in these things called igloos. According to what I seen in this here movie most the folks in Flint is Chinese. Don't believe I seen nan one colored person in the whole dang city. You a 'Bama gal, don't believe you'd be too happy living in no igloo. Ain't got nothing against 'em, but don't believe you'd be too happy living 'mongst a whole slew of Chinese folks. Don't believe you'd like the food. Only thing them Chinese folks in that movie et was whales and seals. Don't believe you'd like no whale meat. Don't taste a lick like chicken. Don't taste like pork at all."

Momma pulled her hand away from her mouth. "Daniel Watson, you are one lying man! Only thing you said that was true was that being in Flint is like living in a igloo. I knew I should have listened to Moses. Maybe these babies mighta been born with lumpy heads but at least they'da had *warm* lumpy heads!

"You know Birmingham is a good place, and I don't mean just the weather either. The life is slower, the people are friendlier—"

"Oh yeah," Dad interrupted, "they're a laugh a minute down there. Let's see, where was that 'Coloreds Only' bathroom downtown?"

"Daniel, you know what I mean, things aren't perfect

but people are more honest about the way they feel"—she took her mean eyes off Dad and put them on Byron—"and folks there do know how to respect their parents."

Byron rolled his eyes like he didn't care. All he did was tuck the blanket farther into the couch's cushion.

Dad didn't like the direction the conversation was going so he called the landlord for the hundredth time. The phone was still busy.

"That snake in the grass has got his phone off the hook. Well, it's going to be too cold to stay here tonight, let me call Cydney. She just had that new furnace put in, maybe we can spend the night there." Aunt Cydney was kind of mean but her house was always warm so we kept our fingers crossed that she was home.

Everyone, even Byron, cheered when Dad got Aunt Cydney and she told us to hurry over before we froze to death.

Dad went out to try and get the Brown Bomber started. That was what we called our car. It was a 1948 Plymouth that was dull brown and real big, Byron said it was turd brown. Uncle Bud gave it to Dad when it was thirteen years old and we'd had it for two years. Me and Dad took real good care of it but some of the time it didn't like to start up in the winter.

After five minutes Dad came back in huffing and puffing and slapping his arms across his chest.

"Well, it was touch and go for a while, but the Great Brown One pulled through again!" Everyone cheered, but me and Byron quit cheering and started frowning right away. By the way Dad smiled at us we knew what was coming next. Dad pulled two ice scrapers out of his pocket and said, "O.K., boys, let's get out there and knock those windows out."

We moaned and groaned and put some more coats on and went outside to scrape the car's windows. I could tell by the way he was pouting that Byron was going to try and get out of doing his share of the work.

"I'm not going to do your part, Byron, you'd better do it and I'm not playing either."

"Shut up, punk."

I went over to the Brown Bomber's passenger side and started hacking away at the scab of ice that was all over the windows. I finished Momma's window and took a break. Scraping ice off of windows when it's that cold can kill you!

I didn't hear any sound coming from the other side of the car so I yelled out, "I'm serious, Byron, I'm not doing that side too, and I'm only going to do half the windshield, I don't care what you do to me." The windshield on the Bomber wasn't like the new 1963 cars, it had a big bar running down the middle of it, dividing it in half.

"Shut your stupid mouth, I got something more important to do right now." •

I peeked around the back of the car to see what By was up to. The only thing he'd scraped off was the outside mirror and he was bending down to look at himself in it. He saw me and said, "You know what, square? I must be adopted, there just ain't no way two folks as ugly as your momma and daddy coulda give birth to someone as sharp as me!"

He was running his hands over his head like he was brushing his hair.

I said, "Forget you," and went back over to the other side of the car to finish the back window. I had half of the ice off when I had to stop again and catch my breath. I heard Byron mumble my name.

I said, "You think I'm stupid? It's not going to work this time." He mumbled my name again. It sounded like his mouth was full of something. I knew this was a trick, I knew this was going to be How to Survive a Blizzard, Part Two.

How to Survive a Blizzard, Part One had been last night when I was outside playing in the snow and Byron and his running buddy, Buphead, came walking by. Buphead has officially been a juvenile delinquent even longer than Byron.

"Say, kid," By had said, "you wanna learn somethin' that might save your stupid life one day?"

I should have known better, but I was bored and I think maybe the cold weather was making my brain slow, so I said, "What's that?"

"We gonna teach you how to survive a blizzard."

"How?"

Byron put his hands in front of his face and said, "This is the most important thing to remember, O.K.?"

"Why?"

"Well, first we gotta show you what it feels like to be trapped in a blizzard. You ready?" He whispered something to Buphead and they both laughed.

"I'm ready."

I should have known that the only reason Buphead and By would want to play with me was to do something mean.

"O.K.," By said, "first thing you gotta worry about is high winds."

Byron and Buphead each grabbed one of my arms and one of my legs and swung me between them going, "*Wooo*, blizzard warnings! Blizzard warnings! *Wooo!* Take cover!"

Buphead counted to three and on the third swing they let me go in the air. I landed headfirst in a snowbank.

But that was O.K. because I had on three coats, two sweaters, a T-shirt, three pairs of pants and four socks along with a scarf, a hat and a hood. These guys couldn't have hurt me if they'd thrown me off the Empire State Building!

After I climbed out of the snowbank they started laughing and so did I.

"Cool, Baby Bruh," By said, "you passed that part of the test with a B-plus, what you think, Buphead?"

Buphead said, "Yeah, I'd give the little punk a A."

They whispered some more and started laughing again.

"O.K.," By said, "second thing you gotta learn is how to keep your balance in a high wind. You gotta be good at this so you don't get blowed into no polar bear dens."

They put me in between them and started making me spin round and round, it seemed like they spun me for about half an hour. When slob started flying out of my mouth they let me stop and I wobbled around for a while before they pushed me back in the same snowbank.

When everything stopped going in circles I got up and we all laughed again.

They whispered some more and then By said, "What you think, Buphead? He kept his balance a good long time, I'm gonna give him a A-minus."

"I ain't as hard a grader as you, I'ma give the little punk a double A-minus."

"O.K., Kenny, now the last part of Surviving a Blizzard, you ready?"

"Yup!"

"You passed the wind test and did real good on the balance test but now we gotta see if you ready to graduate. You remember what we told you was the most important part about survivin'?"

"Yup!"

"O.K., here we go. Buphead, tell him 'bout the final exam."

Buphead turned me around to look at him, putting my back to Byron. "O.K., square," he started, "I wanna make sure you ready for this one, you done so good so far I wanna make sure you don't blow it at graduation time. You think you ready?"

I nodded, getting ready to be thrown in the snow-bank real hard this time. I made up my mind I wasn't going to cry or anything, I made up my mind that no matter how hard they threw me in that snow I was going to get up laughing.

"O.K.," Buphead said, "everything's cool, you 'member what your brother said about puttin' your hands up?"

"Like this?" I covered my face with my gloves.

"Yeah, that's it!" Buphead looked over my shoulder at Byron and then said, "*Wooo!* High winds, blowing snow! *Wooo!* Look out! Blizzard a-comin'! Death around the corner! Look out!"

Byron mumbled my name and I turned around to see why his voice sounded so funny. As soon as I looked at him Byron blasted me in the face with a mouthful of snow.

Man! It was hard to believe how much stuff By could put in his mouth! Him and Buphead just about died laughing as I stood there with snow and spit and ice dripping off of my face.

Byron caught his breath and said, "Aww, man, you flunked! You done so good, then you go and flunk the Blowin' Snow section of How to Survive a Blizzard, you forgot to put your hands up! What you say, Buphead, F?"

"Yeah, double F-minus!"

It was a good thing my face was numb from the cold

already or I might have froze to death. I was too embarrassed about getting tricked to tell on them so I went in the house and watched TV.

So as me and By scraped the ice off the Brown Bomber I wasn't going to get fooled again. I kept on chopping ice off the back window and ignored By's mumbling voice.

The next time I took a little rest Byron was still calling my name but sounding like he had something in his mouth. He was saying, "Keh-ee! Keh-ee! Hel' . . . hel' . . . !" When he started banging on the door of the car I went to take a peek at what was going on.

By was leaned over the outside mirror, looking at something in it real close. Big puffs of steam were coming out of the side of the mirror.

I picked up a big, hard chunk of ice to get ready for Byron's trick.

"Keh-ee! Keh-ee! Hel' me! Hel' me! Go geh Momma! Go geh Mom-ma! Huwwy uh!"

"I'm not playing, Byron! I'm not that stupid! You'd better start doing your side of the car or I'll tear you up with this iceball."

He banged his hand against the car harder and started stomping his feet. "Oh, please, Keh-ee! Hel' me, go geh Mom-ma!"

I raised the ice chunk over my head. "I'm not playing, By, you better get busy or I'm telling Dad."

I moved closer and when I got right next to him I could see boogers running out of his nose and tears running down his cheeks. These weren't tears from the cold either, these were big juicy crybaby tears! I dropped my ice chunk.

"By! What's wrong?"

"Hel' me! Keh-ee! Go geh hel'!"

I moved closer. I couldn't believe my eyes! Byron's mouth was frozen on the mirror! He was as stuck as a fly on flypaper!

I could have done a lot of stuff to him. If it had been me with my lips stuck on something like this he'd have tortured me for a couple of days before he got help. Not me, though, I nearly broke my neck trying to get into the house to rescue Byron.

As soon as I ran through the front door Momma, Dad and Joey all yelled, "Close that door!"

"Momma, quick! It's By! He's froze up outside!"

No one seemed too impressed.

I screamed, "Really! He's froze to the car! Help! He's crying!"

That shook them up. You could cut Byron's head off and he probably wouldn't cry.

"Kenneth Bernard Watson, what on earth are you talking about?"

"Momma, please hurry up!"

Momma, Dad and Joey threw on some extra coats and followed me to the Brown Bomber.

The fly was still stuck and buzzing. "Oh, Mom-ma! Hel' me! Geh me offa 'ere!"

"Oh my Lord!" Momma screamed, and I thought

she was going to do one of those movie-style faints, she even put her hand over her forehead and staggered back a little bit.

Joey, of course, started crying right along with Byron.

Dad was doing his best not to explode laughing. Big puffs of smoke were coming out of his nose and mouth as he tried to squeeze his laughs down. Finally he put his head on his arms and leaned against the car's hood and howled.

"Byron," Momma said, gently wiping tears off his cheeks with the end of her scarf, "it's O.K., sweetheart, how'd this happen?" She sounded like she was going to be crying in a minute herself.

Dad raised his head and said, "Why are you asking how it happened? Can't you tell, Wilona? This little knucklehead was kissing his reflection in the mirror and got his lips stuck!" Dad took a real deep breath. "Is your tongue stuck too?"

"No! Quit teasin', Da-ee! Hel'! Hel'!"

"Well, at least the boy hadn't gotten too passionate with himself!" Dad thought that was hilarious and put his head back on his arms.

Momma didn't see anything funny. "Daniel Watson! What are we gonna do?